THE MAN WHO WAS THURSDAY

The Man Who Was Thursday

Adapted from the novel by G. K. Chesterton

ISBN-13: 978-1944540425
ISBN-10: 1944540423

For information about production rights, contact:
bilald@gmail.com

Published by Sordelet Ink
WWW.SORDELETINK.COM

Cover by David Blixt

THE MAN WHO WAS THURSDAY

A PLAY IN FOUR ACTS

BY

BILAL DARDAI

ADAPTED FROM THE NOVEL BY

G.K. CHESTERTON

SORDELET
Link

The Man Who Was Thursday received its world-premiere production from New Leaf Theatre in Chicago, Illinois (Jess Hutchinson, Artistic Director) from October 15 to November 21, 2009, directed by Jess Hutchinson. The set design was by Michelle Lilly with additional original artwork by Marni Keenan, sound design by Nick Keenan, lighting design by Jared Moore, costume design by Rachel Sypniewski, dialect coaching by Lindsay Bartlett, and violence design by Greg Poljacik. Dramaturgy was by Jacob Juntunen and stage management was by Amanda Frechette. The cast was as follows:

SYME — Dan Granata
GREGORY — Nick Mikula
SECRETARY — Nate Burger
GOGOL — T. Patrick Halley
MARQUIS — Brian Rooney
DE WORMS — Andy Hager
DR. BULL — Ted Evans
SUNDAY — Sean Patrick Fawcett
ENSEMBLE — Joel Ewing, Austin Oie

The newly revised version of the script was produced by Lifeline Theatre (Ilesa Duncan, Artistic Director) in Chicago, Illinois, from February 15 to April 7, 2019, directed by Jess Hutchinson. The set design was by Lizzie Bracken, sound design and original compositions by Christopher Kriz, lighting design by Eric Watkins, props design by Jenny Pinson, costume/makeup design by Caitlin McLeod & Anna Wooden, dialect coaching by Elise Kauzlaric, and violence design by Greg Poljacik. Dramaturgy was by Zev Valancy and stage management by Amanda Beranek. The cast was as follows:

SYME — Eduardo Xavier Curley-Carillo
GREGORY — Cory Hardin
SECRETARY — Marsha Harman
GOGOL — Christopher M. Walsh
MARQUIS — Corrbette Pasko
DE WORMS — Linsey Falls
DR. BULL — Jen Ellison
SUNDAY — Allison Cain
ENSEMBLE — Sonia Goldberg, Oly Oxinfry

For information about production rights, contact:
bilald@gmail.com

Cast of Characters

Gabriel SYME
Lucian GREGORY
The SECRETARY (Monday)
GOGOL (Tuesday)
The MARQUIS de St. Eustache (Wednesday)
Professor DE WORMS (Friday)
DR. BULL (Saturday)
SUNDAY

ENSEMBLE

Setting

EUROPE, EARLY 1900s

A NOTE ON CASTING

The Man Who Was Thursday is written for 25 distinct roles (8 principal, 17 ensemble). In its initial productions, many of these ensemble roles were distributed among both certain principals and two additional swing performers, allowing the play to be performed with as few as 10 actors. Future productions are welcome to deviate from this number as they are able and as they see fit.

Although the play is set in 1908 Europe it is not beholden to history. Rather, it is a play about deceptions, disguises, theatricality, and haphazard definitions of truth. The author encourages productions to cast inclusively—but also consciously—across spectrums of race and gender.

ACT I

SCENE ONE

(Saffron Park, a suburb on the west side of London, just before dusk, in the year 1908. Street lamps dimly lit and a bench on the sidewalk. The sound of somebody practicing a piano from a distant parlor. Members of the ENSEMBLE stroll along the sidewalk, speaking casually to each other—in this scene, the ENSEMBLE will be the CROWD. One of these people is GABRIEL SYME, a smartly dressed gentleman in his late twenties, wearing a top hat and holding a walking stick. When a large crowd has gathered onstage, LUCIAN GREGORY, a man with a severe manner, steps upon the bench and holds aloft a stick of dynamite. He proclaims loudly, getting everybody's attention at once)

GREGORY
This!

(Everybody except for SYME looks at GREGORY and freezes. SYME speaks to the audience)

SYME

You must know this: it had been a beautiful day. I speak to you here as a poet, who understands such things. A beautiful day. Clear, cloudless…the sky vast and open, painted in symphonic shades of blue. The gardens taking great breaths of that crisp, clean air; the people walking the streets in robust paragraphs…this was Saffron Park, and even if night's bony fingers now crept over the horizon, the day…had been beautiful. It is important to remember beautiful days, if only to be reminded that, after all is said and done, such days will come again. You must know this.

(He turns to look at GREGORY. The scene resumes)

GREGORY

This! *(He makes sure all eyes are upon him before continuing.)*

> This is a tale of those old fears,
>> Even of those emptied hells,
> And none but you shall understand
>> The true thing that it tells—
> Of what colossal gods of shame
>> Could cow men and yet crash
> Of what huge devils hid the stars,
>> Yet fell at a pistol flash.
> The doubts that were so plain to chase,
>> So dreadful to withstand—
> Oh who shall understand but you;
>> Yes, who shall understand?

(He finishes, holding the dynamite in a triumphant manner. After a moment, the crowd begins to clap with polite approval. GREGORY bows)

CROWD #1
Back again, Lucian! How nice to see our vaga-
bond poet return!

CROWD #2
It's been what, a week, since last we heard you?
The air has been positively empty without your
indictments.

GREGORY
You would say that the air is empty? I say our air
is oppression, for our air is shared by oppressors.
Does Buckingham Palace stand? Does Parliament
still assemble? English air will not be empty,
madam, until that air is truly free.

CROWD #3
Then recite more verse, Mr. Gregory! Liberate
the air! Tell us more of your noble rebellion!

*(The CROWD laughs. GREGORY pulls the cap
off of the stick of dynamite and removes a rolled-
up piece of paper)*

GREGORY
Simpletons. You think I speak to you of "rebellion"? Rebellion is for wayward children. I am
no rebel; I am an artist. I am an anarchist. For
poetry is anarchy, and anarchy poetry, and only
within each other may they exist! *(He unrolls
the piece of paper and prepares to recite)* "The
fire—"

SYME
(interrupting) I beg your pardon.

GREGORY
(taken aback) What? Yes? Who was that?

SYME
(stepping forward from the crowd) That was me.

GREGORY
And you are...?

SYME
I am a poet, like yourself.

(A slight murmur through the CROWD)

GREGORY
A poet, you say?

SYME
A poet I did say, yes...but permit a retraction. I am a poet, but in fact nothing like yourself; for I absolutely must differ with you on the nature of poetry. You claim that poetry and anarchy are one and the same. I claim that cannot be, as I stand before you a poet of law, and of order...nay, a poet of respectability.

(A louder murmur through the CROWD. GREGORY hesitates but a moment)

GREGORY
Forgive my hesitation, Mr...?

SYME
Syme, sir. Gabriel Syme.

GREGORY
So a respectable poet walks among us, somehow unheralded by earthquakes, or by comets in the sky. You say you are a poet of law? I say you are a contradiction in terms!

SYME
Truly?

GREGORY
An artist is identical with an anarchist! The man
who dares throw a bomb is an artist, because
he prefers a great moment to everything. He
knows how much more valuable is one burst of
blazing light, one peal of perfect thunder, than
the common bodies of a few shapeless states-
men. An artist disregards governance! Abolishes
conventions! Delights in disorder and the death
of routine! A poet of order? If it were so, the
most poetical thing in the world would be the
Underground Railway.

SYME
So it is.

GREGORY
Nonsense! Why do all the passengers look so
sad and tired? Because they know that the train
is going right, that whatsoever place they have
bought a ticket for, that place they must reach.
After Sloane Square, there must be Victoria, and
nothing but Victoria. Imagine their rapture, if just
once, the next station were unaccountably Baker
Street!

SYME
It is you who are being un-poetical. The strange
thing is to hit the mark; the gross and obvious
thing is to miss it. It is impressive when a man
with one arrow strikes a distant bird. Is it not also
impressive when with one roaring flailing beast
of an engine he strikes a distant station? *(Beat)*
Chaos is dull, Mr. Gregory. In chaos a train might
go to Baker Street or Baghdad and neither destination has any more meaning than the other. But

the magician that is man, he says "Victoria," and lo! It is Victoria.

GREGORY
You would ascribe poetry to a timetable!

SYME
I would. Every time my train comes in it's as if I've won a battle with fate itself. After I leave Sloane Square, I might come to Victoria, true, but a thousand other things might also happen. To arrive at one's destination, safely, on time; by all propriety one ought to compose an epic to the journey. Indeed, I feel the start of one now. *(He recites a poem with an offhanded confidence, directly contrasting GREGORY's previous bombast)*

> What vicious claws have fire and time
> > To tear and rend asunder!
> Yet how the hands of engineers
> > Might tame their deadly thunder.
> Do angels perch within mine ears
> > To craft my benedictory?
> The conductor shouts "Vic-tor-i-a!"
> > And I hear it still as "Victory!"

(The CROWD is both amused and delighted by the performance. GREGORY is visibly nonplussed. CROWD applauds)

SYME
No, no, please. A mere whimsical trifle, that.

GREGORY
Victory, you say. What is your victory? Some new and peaceful Eden? But then to know that such an Eden is nothing more than a lifeless train station. Yes, a poet will ever be discontented, even walk-

ing the streets of heaven. The poet is always in revolt—!

SYME
—revolt? What is poetical about revolt? Being seasick is a revolt. Being sick and being rebellious may have their utility on certain desperate occasions, but I'm hanged if I can see why they are poetry. Revolt as you call it, in the abstract, is merely...vomiting.

GREGORY
Sir...

SYME
That which goes right is poetry. The digestion of our meals, the verses of our viscera, these are the foundations of poetry! Yes, moreso than flowers, or stars! The most poetic thing is not to be sick.

GREGORY
Really...these examples you choose are hardly...

SYME
I beg your pardon. I thought we had abolished all conventions.

(Pause. The CROWD looks to GREGORY)

GREGORY
Am I expected to revolutionize the whole of society from a park bench?

SYME
Of course not. *(He sits casually on the bench)* But if you were serious about your anarchism, that is exactly what you would do.

(Pause. GREGORY is stunned)

GREGORY
(fuming) You think...that I am not serious?

SYME
Hm?

GREGORY
(livid) You believe I am not serious about my anarchism?!

SYME
(dismissively) My dear fellow.

(SYME remains on the bench, calmly, ignoring GREGORY. GREGORY looks from SYME to the CROWD, to London, to the bench, completely lost in his fury. The CROWD departs, leaving the two of them alone. GREGORY plops down on the bench, very nearly pouting. A very long, uncomfortable pause. The sunlight fades away, the streetlights brighten)

GREGORY
Mr. Syme.

SYME
Yes, Mr. Gregory.

GREGORY
This evening you have done something remarkable. Something that no man has ever succeeded in doing before. You have irritated me.

SYME
I am very sorry.

GREGORY
No apology can overcome my fury. No duel would suffice; if I were to strike you dead your insult

would remain. My only satisfaction would be to prove to you—at the possible sacrifice of my life and honor—that you are wrong in your accusations. I am serious about being an anarchist. In a deeper sense, a more…deadly sense, am I serious.

SYME
Deadly serious, you say. All things die, Mr. Gregory. Ruin and decay are painfully ordinary. A man may stand in a crowd and speak very well indeed, filled to the top of his skull with drink or religion, but why should they be considered any more serious than a loosened cobblestone, a flickering streetlamp, the whole damned caboodle? Seriousness has degrees, sir. You have an abundance of sincerity. It's your conviction I hold in doubt.

GREGORY
(standing) Very well. You shall see something more serious than either drink or religion. But first I must ask you to swear.

SYME
An oath? To whom?

GREGORY
To whatever gods or saints may inhabit your creed of order, swear that you will not reveal what I am going to show you. To no man, and especially to no policeman. Make only this vow to me, and I will promise you, in return…*(He trails off)*

SYME
You promise me…?

GREGORY
A very entertaining evening.

SYME

Your offer, Mr. Gregory, is far too idiotic to be declined. We may disagree when a poet is an anarchist, but I would hope that a poet is always a sportsman. I will promise you as a good Englishman and a fellow artist that I will not report anything of this, whatever this is, to the police. Now what the devil is it?

GREGORY

(walks offstage, beckoning) This way, Mr. Syme.

(They exit. Lights down)

END ACT I, SCENE ONE

Scene Two

(*A round table in a bar parlor. GREGORY leads SYME to the table, and they sit. A WAITER stands silently near the table, half in darkness*)

GREGORY
Supper?

SYME
Certainly.

GREGORY
And to drink? The scotch is quite to be trusted.

SYME
As you say.

GREGORY
(*to the WAITER, with purpose*) Lobster mayonnaise, a crème de menthe, and a fifth of scotch.

(*WAITER exits, acknowledging the phrase*)

SYME
Lobster?

GREGORY
Scavenger creatures, fed only to convicts. We would not presume to deserve better.

SYME
And this we would be...

GREGORY
The serious anarchists.

(WAITER returns with a plate of lobster salad, and the drinks. The WAITER stands back into the shadows)

SYME
Serious about your meals, for starters.

GREGORY
We are serious about everything. Cigar? *(He offers one from within his jacket)*

(SYME takes one and lights it. GREGORY does the same. They smoke in silence, SYME also drinking his scotch and eating his lobster. The WAITER may be seen pushing a button or pulling a lever. There is a loud whooshing noise, and the parlor suddenly disappears, save for a single light on the table from above. SYME looks up into it. Pause)

SYME
May I ask.

GREGORY
Please do.

SYME
Was it the lobster that you poisoned?

GREGORY
No.

SYME
The scotch, then.

GREGORY
No. You were not poisoned.

(The light from above is covered up, leaving the two men and the table in darkness)

SYME
Then I can only deduce our table has plummeted several meters below the earth into a dark pit?

GREGORY
It has.

SYME
That is a relief.

GREGORY
(lights a match) Follow me, please.

(Through the next exchange, GREGORY and SYME may travel anywhere in the theater. GREGORY will periodically light matches as they travel, dropping any that go out and then lighting another)

GREGORY
Are you beginning to understand my seriousness yet, sir?

SYME
I understand nothing. Subterranean tunnels speak to very many peculiar character traits, but I do not believe that serious anarchism is one of them.

GREGORY
We are not there yet. You will see, once we are there.

SYME
Mind you, this is a very unusual environment for any mere poet to inhabit. Excepting, perhaps, Byron...

GREGORY
Suffice to say that I am breaking a very strict oath of secrecy in bringing you here. I can't explain to you in any sensible way why I have done it; it's one of those arbitrary emotions, like jumping off a cliff or falling in love. But you, sir, have so intolerably irritated me that I would break twenty such oaths for the pleasure of taking you down a peg.

SYME
You flatter me. In better light, I am sure you would see me flush with embarrassment.

(They travel in silence for a moment)

SYME
So this is how one goes about abolishing government, then?

GREGORY
No, this is how one goes about abolishing God!

(They are standing onstage again. There is suddenly a wash of white light, and they are standing in a cold, black room. There is a large, round, wooden council table in the center, and the back wall is covered with ball-shaped bombs and miscellaneous firearms. It is a very impressive arsenal. There is a cloak, revolver, and sword-stick on the table. GREGORY pauses for effect)

SYME
How festive.

GREGORY
To abolish God, Mr. Syme. There is more to
true anarchy than to pull down despots and defy
police regulations...we dig deeper. We erupt
higher. We deny all distinctions of vice and
virtue, honor and treachery, those base ideas that
fuel common rebels. The silly sentimentalists of
the French Revolution, how they screamed and
shed blood over the so-called Rights of Man! We
hate Rights and we hate Wrongs. We will abolish
Right and Wrong.

SYME
And you will also abolish Right and Left, I hope?
I find those far more troublesome.

GREGORY
Still you mock! Still! Even at...all this...!

SYME
No no, this is most impressive! Were I God, I
would feel half-abolished already at the sight of
it. *(He removes his hat and bows)* I stand corrected,
Mr. Gregory. Clearly we should all have trusted
you when you confessed to be a heinous bomb-
throwing fiend.

GREGORY
The dull skepticism of the masses is to be
expected. In fact, I rely upon it. That is the
genius of Sunday.

SYME
I beg your pardon? Sunday?

GREGORY
The President of our Central Anarchist Council.
There are seven on this council, who are named

after days of the week. Sunday is their leader, and ours.

SYME
A clever nomenclature.

GREGORY
A clever man. A great and terrible man.

SYME
Yet how peculiar that such a man remains unknown to the common citizen.

GREGORY
Caesar and Napoleon put all their effort into being heard of, and they were heard of. Sunday puts all of his effort into not being heard of, and he is not. But one cannot spend five minutes in a room with him without feeling that those emperors would have been children in his hands. *(Beat)* An example. I asked him, Sunday, how I should disguise myself in society so as not to arouse suspicion. I had attempted to pass as a priest, and then as an army major...and neither charade was convincing. I understand now. Sunday made me understand. "You want a safe disguise?" he asked me. "To have nobody expect anything dangerous of you? Then dress up as an anarchist, you fool!"

SYME
It is a good ruse. Indeed, for as harmless as you appear, you must conversely be the most serious of anarchists.

GREGORY
I'm pleased to hear you say that. *(Beat)* May I share another secret with you, Syme?

SYME
Another? I shall be overladen.

GREGORY
Tonight, in this very room, there is to be a special
session to fill a vacancy on the Central Council.
The gentleman who had for some time assumed
the role of Thursday has died quite suddenly,
and a successor must be appointed immediately.
There is a formal election, of course, but I don't
mind telling you...it is almost certain that I am
to be Thursday.

SYME
Then I congratulate you! A great career!

GREGORY
(giddily) A short ceremony, I am sure...I will take
up the cloak and arms here upon the table, and
then out of this cavern to a steam-ship waiting
on the river, which will take me to the Council
and then—and then—oh, the wild joy of being
Thursday!

SYME
What an utterly likeable human being you are,
Mr. Gregory! I am sure you will make a most
pleasant villain!

GREGORY
I thank you. You have been gracious in your defeat.

SYME
Not at all. This is by far the funniest situation I've
been in in my life, and I am going to act accord-
ingly, by God! I made you a vow of secrecy upon
entering this realm of yours; would you give me,
for my own safety, a similar promise?

GREGORY
A promise?

SYME
For as I have sworn not to reveal your secret to
the police, would you now promise not to reveal
my secret to the anarchists?

GREGORY
You have a secret?

SYME
I do. Will you swear?

(Pause)

GREGORY
This damnable…curiosity…of artists! Yes, I will
swear. I will not tell the anarchists what you tell
me. But be quick about it, they will be here in
a few minutes.

SYME
Well. I don't know how to tell you the truth in
a more expedient manner than to say to you that
your trick of dressing as a mercurial poet is not
unheard of outside of your circle. In fact, we
have known the dodge for some time at Scotland
Yard.

(A very awkward silence)

GREGORY
What.

SYME
Yes. I am a police detective. Ah! I hear your
friends coming.

(The sound of the ANARCHISTS murmuring in

the theater can be heard, growing slowly louder.
GREGORY grabs the revolver off the table and
points it at SYME)

SYME
Really, sir, do not be hasty.

GREGORY
But! I...a detective! You dare to...! I...!

SYME
Can't you see we're in the same boat? And jolly
seasick, to boot!

GREGORY
I'll see you dead!

SYME
Think, man! We've checkmated each other. I'm
a policeman bereft of the aid of the police, and
you are an anarchist unable to reveal my identity
without implicating yourself as well. Shoot me
now, and you will probably find yourself beset
upon with all manner of questions from your
fellows, and it may be revealed that you unwit-
tingly allowed me into your inner sanctum. At
which point, I would hazard, it would be fortunate if you were merely denied the position of
Thursday. *(Beat)* But take heart! The advantage is
clearly yours—you are not surrounded by police,
but I am surrounded by anarchists.

GREGORY
So you propose—what, exactly? You shall attend
our meeting and then simply go along your
merry way?

SYME
Precisely.

GREGORY
On your merry way back to Scotland Yard!

SYME
Did I not make you a vow?

(Pause. GREGORY is very confused)

GREGORY
You intend to...honor your promise?

SYME
Naturally.

GREGORY
But—!

SYME
—Mr. Gregory, you and I are representatives of a much larger struggle, that between order and chaos. I daresay that I have faith that my side will prevail well enough without such dishonorable behavior on my part. There is no need to bump the billiard table. Do you not have the same conviction in your philosophy? I thought we were serious.

Pause. GREGORY puts the revolver back on the table.

SYME
Good show, sir.

(The ANARCHISTS enter the room from all sides available. They are dressed in black, cruel overcoats. They take seats at the table, whispering to each other. One of these men is BUTTONS. He holds a small legal folder filled with paper, and approaches SYME and GREGORY suspiciously)

BUTTONS
Comrade Gregory.

GREGORY
(nervously) Well met, Comrade Buttons.

BUTTONS
And is this man a delegate?

GREGORY
Er...yes, a delegate.

SYME
Your gate is so well guarded, sir; it would be hard
for anybody who was not a delegate to be here.
(Extends his hand) Gabriel Syme.

BUTTONS
And which branch do you represent?

SYME
No branch. Moreso a root. *(Beat)* You might call
me a Sabbatarian. I am here to see that you show
a due observance of Sunday.

*(All whispering abruptly stops, and the
ANARCHISTS look at SYME. BUTTONS drops
his folder, and then abruptly scurries to pick the
papers up)*

BUTTONS
I...oh...I see. We should...of course...we should
give you a seat at the meeting?

SYME
Oh, I think you'd better.

*(There is a mad scramble to get a seat for SYME.
He directs it off to the side, away from the cluster at
the table. Everybody watches him, anxious, as he sits.*

Finally, he nods to the ANARCHISTS and observes, quietly. GREGORY watches all of this with frustration. BUTTONS stands at the head of table, standing on a step slightly higher than the ANARCHISTS)

BUTTONS
It is...ahem. It is time we began. The steamship is waiting already. Our meeting tonight is important, but it need not be long. It is the honor of this branch to select a new Thursday. We all lament the passing of the heroic worker who occupied that chair until last week. His services to the cause were considerable. Most notably, as you all remember, he organized the dynamite coup of Brighton, which, under happier circumstances, would have killed everybody on the pier.

ANARCHISTS
Hear, hear!

BUTTONS
But alas, we are not here to acclaim the virtues of that worthy dynamiter, but for the harder task of replacing him. Out of our company here tonight, we must unanimously select the man who would be Thursday. Present a nominee and we shall put him to the vote.

ANARCHIST #1
(standing) I move that Comrade Gregory be elected Thursday.

BUTTONS
Second?

ANARCHIST #2
Second.

BUTTONS
Lucian! Please approach.

(GREGORY walks quickly to BUTTONS' side)

BUTTONS
Before we vote, I ask that our nominee make a statement. Do you have one prepared?

GREGORY
I do. *(He pulls a speech from his jacket and orates to the ANARCHISTS)* My brothers in gunpowder. I do not need to explain my policy. It is your policy. We have been slandered in society, our aims have been misinterpreted and disfigured. People learn of anarchism from six-penny novels, or from newspapers, or from half-wit conversations in hotel parlors. They never learn anarchy from anarchists. And why, I ask you? Because we are persecuted. Because we are demonized by those ignorant masses above us, who fail to understand the better world we are trying to create. No more, say I! As your Thursday, I will destroy the walls within the mind of society as well as the walls without. I will blow their eyes open! They will see at last what anarchy offers, they will see that we are more than murderers and enemies of human society. There will be no slander—we will pursue with courage, and intellectual pressure, the permanent ideals of brotherhood that are inherent in anarchy. I thank you for your confidence, comrades.

(GREGORY stands before them, beaming. There is a smattering of polite applause and murmuring. BUTTONS steps next to GREGORY, smiling halfheartedly)

BUTTONS
Yes. Well. Good speech, anyway. Ahem. *(To the ANARCHISTS)* Does anyone oppose the election of Comrade Gregory?

(A moment of quiet discussion among the ANARCHISTS. The air is of resignation)

SYME
Yes, Mr. Buttons. I oppose.

(Everybody looks over)

BUTTONS
The Chair recognizes Mr. Syme?

(SYME stands and continues in a loud and clear voice. He walks over to the table during his speech, pushing next to GREGORY on the step, and ultimately moves to the tabletop. The ANARCHISTS voice approval where appropriate)

SYME
Have we come here for this? Do we meet underground like rats, cover our walls with bombs and bar our door with death, for such milquetoast offering as this? "Courage and intellectual pressure?" "The better world we will create?" These are fine words, yes, if one is an archbishop. If one were an archbishop, I am sure they would have listened to Comrade Gregory's words with great pleasure! But I am not an archbishop, my friends, and I did not find any pleasure in his words. Our dear Mr. Gregory may have found pleasure in his words, and as such he may one day make a fine archbishop...but the man who is fit to be an archbishop is not fit to be a serious anarchist. He is not fit to be a forcible and efficient Thursday.

GREGORY
Now see here...

SYME
He tells us in the most apologetic tone that we are not the enemies of society. I say that we are the enemies of society, and so much the worse for society! We are society's oldest and most pitiless enemy! We are the Anarchist! We are not murderers, true, as Mr. Gregory points out. We are executioners.

(The ANARCHISTS cheer)

GREGORY
(stepping onto the table with SYME) You...you damnable hypocrite!

SYME
Hypocrite, am I? He knows as well as I do that I am keeping all of my vows; doing nothing but my duty. I will not mince words. I say that Comrade Gregory, for all his amiable qualities, is not fit to be Thursday. I say that he is unfit because of all his amiable qualities. Should the Central Council be a place for ceremonial politeness and modesty? I set myself against his election as I set myself against all the governments of Europe, because the man who has truly embraced anarchy has forgotten modesty. He has forgotten pride! Am I a man? No! I am a cause! I am as impersonal and resolute as one of the weapons on this wall, and I say that rather than have Gregory and his sentimentality infect the Central Council, I would offer up myself for election—!

(The ANARCHISTS rise as one and applaud)

GREGORY
Stop! Stop, you madmen!

SYME
I will not rebut the slander that we are murderers,
I will earn it! To the priest who condemns our
souls, to the judge who condemns our bodies, to
the fat Parliamentarian who condemns our spirits,
I would grip their throats and cry FALSE KINGS
OF SOCIETY, MY NAME IS THURSDAY, AND
I COME TO DESTROY YOU!

*(The ANARCHISTS are in frenzy. GREGORY
is forcibly pulled off the table and pushed to the
outside of the circle)*

BUTTONS
Order! Order, anarchists, ORDER!

ANARCHIST #3
I move that Comrade Syme be elected to the
post!

GREGORY
You cannot—!

ANARCHISTS
—Second!

GREGORY
Enough! Enough of this! This man cannot be
elected, he is—

SYME
—Yes. What is he?

Pause. They stare at GREGORY.

GREGORY
He is...inexperienced...in our particular branch.

(Pause. They turn away from GREGORY)

BUTTONS
We shall move to the matter of appointment. All in favor of Comrade Syme?

(GREGORY rushes the table and stands upon it once more, next to a calm SYME)

GREGORY
Comrades! You must hear me! DO NOT ELECT THIS MAN! Call it madness if you must, but act upon it! Strike me down but hear my command! Kill me! But by all that we hold dear, OBEY ME!

A cold silence. The ANARCHISTS stare at GREGORY. SYME meets GREGORY'S eyes, but simply straightens his clothes and says nothing.

ANARCHISTS
(many of them grumbling) Command...command...? Obey, he says...obey my command...of all the... obey, he says...

ANARCHIST #4
(standing) Comrade Gregory commands?

ANARCHIST #5
(standing) Who are you? You are not Sunday.

ANARCHIST #6
(standing) And you...are not Thursday.

BUTTONS
(quietly pulling GREGORY from the table) Really, comrade. This is not dignified. *(To the assembly)* In favor of Comrade Syme for Thursday?

ANARCHISTS
Aye!

BUTTONS
(hands SYME the revolver and sword-stick)
The motion is carried. May you do the post
of Thursday proud, sir. *(He takes the cloak and
drapes it over SYME'S shoulders)* Now, comrades,
to the river! We must send off our new Thursday
in all of the lusty manner that defines our class!

ANARCHISTS
Hurrah!

*(They rise and exit in one direction, save for
GREGORY. SYME stays and looks at him)*

SYME
You overestimate them, you see.

GREGORY
Do not speak to me, villain.

SYME
You are a poet, and so you remain trapped in that
most indelible quality of all poets.

GREGORY
Which would be?

SYME
Idealism. You wish to destroy the world, true, but in
doing so you hope to make it better. You believed
the people in this chamber shared your purposes.
They do not. They wish to destroy the world for
no other purpose than to destroy the world.

GREGORY
What shall we do now?

SYME
Now? I take it I must step aboard some wretched
steam-ship and do my best to keep my lobster

down. It is unfortunate that you anarchists are so opposed to the Underground Railway.

GREGORY
Then you shall not go to Scotland Yard?

SYME
How many times must I make that promise, sir?

GREGORY
And you trust me, even now, not to reveal your identity?

SYME
Now it is far too late, you must agree. Now any such accusation would appear to be little more than spite. *(Beat)* Still, I am grateful to you. It is exactly as you promised, Mr. Gregory.

GREGORY
Promised?!

SYME
It has been a very entertaining evening.

(SYME tips his hat and exits. GREGORY is left alone onstage, fuming)

END ACT I

ACT II

SCENE ONE

(SYME speaks to the audience in an isolated spot-light)

SYME
And who, we now ask, is this fellow Gabriel Syme? In the short time we have known him, the man has claimed to be a poet, a policeman, and now Supreme Anarchist Thursday. He may next say that he is a zookeeper, and then shift again, and purport to be one of the elephants! If this man Syme were to assure you that, once upon a time, he was not wont to such dramatic shifts of character, how could you believe him? How can a man of such transience be trusted at anything he says? *(Beat)* Such is the conundrum of chaos. It cannot be trusted to be anything other than itself, but itself...may be anything. *(Beat)* Listen to the policeman wax poetic, you think! The mystery is solved. This Syme is surely a world-weary veteran of the constabulary, moved to

philosophy by the experiences of his career. In fact, he could hardly be considered a veteran, nor did the world weary him. Only a few short months ago, he had been a poet as coarse and angry as that unfortunate Mr. Gregory—albeit a poet who thought the world was an invigorating experiment, worth preserving. But this was an era rampant with assassins and saboteurs, and the poet's nerves were in tatters from the anticipation of violence, by the injustice of explosions for which nobody had been made to answer. A man shrieking his poor and forgettable verse into the fog, demanding that the police do something, do anything at all...! *(Beat. He removes from his waistcoat pocket a small blue card)* So they did. They recruited him. *(He puts the card away)* They brought him to an old station house and placed him in a darkened room, and out of that void an unseen voice:

VOICE
(offstage, booming) Are you the new recruit?

SYME
(to the VOICE, as if in front of him) I beg your pardon?

VOICE
Would you set yourself against the assembled forces of anarchy currently festering in the skin of our great Europe?

SYME
I would, but—

VOICE
—then you are engaged. Welcome to the law, Mr. Syme.

SYME
I really have no experience.

VOICE
Nobody has experience...in the battle of Armageddon.

SYME
Surely I am unfit to—

VOICE
—you are willing. That is enough.

SYME
I know of no profession where mere willingness is the only requirement.

VOICE
There is. Martyr. You are condemned to death. Good day.

(The spotlight disappears. Darkness onstage. SYME lights a match, and with it, lights a small lantern. The lights onstage begin to slowly, almost imperceptibly, brighten, as if gradually becoming lit by sunrise)

SYME
And with little more than that, Gabriel Syme was a detective. In troubled times, of course, there is need to act swiftly, if one is to act at all. Better to light a lantern than to curse the darkness.

(The SECRETARY appears from the audience, also brandishing a lantern. She is both officious and efficient in demeanor, carrying a legal ledger under one arm and a pocket watch on a chain. She calls to SYME, walking towards the stage and checking her watch)

SECRETARY
Thursday.

SYME
That I am.

SECRETARY
Right on schedule. If we walk to Leicester Square,
we shall be just in time for breakfast. Sunday
insisted on an early breakfast. Have you had any
sleep?

SYME
No.

SECRETARY
Nor I. I shall attempt to sleep after breakfast.

SYME
This is typical?

SECRETARY
Sunday is an early riser. Truth be told, I have no
proof that Sunday sleeps at all. Come now.

*(SYME steps off of the stage and follows the
SECRETARY out of the theater)*

SYME
Which of us are you, then?

SECRETARY
I am the Council Secretary. You will know me as
Monday.

SYME
Sunday's immediate follower?

SECRETARY
As are we all, sir.

(They exit. There is now the light of early morning onstage. The scene has been set. A tablecloth is draped over the round table, and seven chairs are placed around it in a half-circle. The railing of a balcony is placed behind the table. Plates, silverware, and glasses are set. There is a large breakfast feast on the table—breads, bacon, eggs, fruit, etcetera. The sky in the background is blue and cloudy, like an impressionist oil painting.

Three seats are unoccupied. The other four contain their appropriate inhabitants, each a distinctive character.

Occupying the seat of Friday is Professor DE WORMS, an ancient, stooped man in tweed with a weary red flower in the lapel of his jacket.

Occupying the seat of Wednesday is the MARQUIS de St. Eustache, a well-dressed man of noble carriage and an elegant goatee. He toys with a small dagger.

Occupying the seat of Tuesday is GOGOL, a man dressed very well in white shirt and tie, but whose face is a mess of shaggy hair and beard. He has an overwrought Polish accent.

Occupying the seat of Saturday is DR. BULL, an icy individual wearing large, round, impenetrable black spectacles. He barely seems alive.

And there is SUNDAY at center, standing with his back to the room, looking over the balcony, smoking a large cigar. He is a massive individual with white hair)

GOGOL
(standing) Zis is more like it! Ze open air! Enough

of zese games of goncealment, I zay. Let ze world know who we are, zat vhat we would zay is too important to zpeak in dark boxes!

DE WORMS
Comrade Gogol, please.

SUNDAY
(still turned away) Our friend Tuesday doesn't grasp the idea. He dresses up as a gentleman but thinks himself too great a soul to behave like one. He is little more than a stage conspirator, a man who says to others "I am one of the respectable class," and then turns to some unseen audience and says "Aha! In truth I am a villain." *(He turns around)* A man may go about London in a top hat and coat, and nobody would need know he is an anarchist. But if that man then crawls about on his hands and knees, he will attract attention. That is what our Mr. Gogol does. He goes about like an animal with such exhaustive diplomacy that on mornings like this he finds it impossible to walk upright.

GOGOL
I am not ashamed of ze cause. I am not good at goncealment.

SUNDAY
Nobody accuses you of shame, you great ass. I'm speaking of your failure to grasp the aesthetic. Listen: If a man finds a hairy vagrant hiding under his bed, brandishing an instrument of murder, he may pause to note the circumstance. But if he finds a gentleman in a top hat there instead, you will agree with me, my dear Tuesday...that even should he survive the encounter, he is unlikely

ever to forget it. *(Beat)* Now, when you were discovered under Admiral Biffin's bed…

GOGOL
(flustered) I…it was…I am not good at…deception.

SUNDAY
Right, my boy, right. You're not good at much of anything. *(Beat)* You suppose we're up on this balcony so that the world can get a better earful of you? We are up here because it makes it easier for the world to ignore us. "Listen to the silly men talk. They laugh and say they will throw bombs at the king."

(SYME and the SECRETARY have entered the scene during this exchange)

SUNDAY
Am I right, Comrade Monday?

(The others turn to SYME and the SECRETARY)

SECRETARY
We are the very object of ridicule.

SUNDAY
Mm. This our Thursday?

SECRETARY
He is.

SUNDAY
Then why is he standing on ceremony? Introduce the man and let him eat something. He'll think us cruel.

SECRETARY
(indicating each person in turn) Gentlemen, this is

Gabriel Syme, our new Thursday. Mr. Syme, these are, at present order, the Professor De Worms, who occupies the seat of Friday; the Marquis de St. Eustache, our most able Wednesday; Comrade Gogol of Poland—

GOGOL
(interrupting) —ze Polish are most skilled at zis vork—

SECRETARY
(ignoring him) —and at the end, our illustrious Saturday the Dr. Bull. And of course... *(indicates SUNDAY)*

SYME
...of course.

SUNDAY
(referring to the seats) I apologize for the organization of our unhappy calendar.

SYME
There is no need. If one intends to abolish society, they may well begin with the abolition of chronology.

(Pause)

SUNDAY
(laughs heartily) You're going to fit in just fine, Brother Thursday.

(SYME and the SECRETARY sit in their appropriate chairs. For the rest of this conversation, each individual sits and partakes of breakfast. Periodically, SUNDAY will stare at SYME, making him visibly uncomfortable)

SECRETARY
Might I inquire as to the progress of Amsterdam?

DR. BULL
On schedule.

SECRETARY
Oxford?

DE WORMS
Difficult.

SECRETARY
Impossible?

DE WORMS
I never said that.

SECRETARY
Very well. Admiral Biffin?

GOGOL
Ah…

SECRETARY
Never mind. *(Beat)* Which leaves us with Paris, still.

MARQUIS
It will be a thing of beauty.

SECRETARY
Then our information was accurate.

MARQUIS
The Czar, and Le President of France, they will be meeting in three days time. How unfortunate for them. It will be glorious, their assassination. It will be opera. *(Beat)* I have wondered often, however, whether it wouldn't be better if

I did it with a knife. A great many things have been brought off with a knife. And it would be a new emotion, yes, to get a knife into a French President and wriggle it round.

SECRETARY
Respectfully, my comrade the Marquis, you are wrong. A knife is outmoded; the expression of personal quarrels with personal tyrants. Dynamite is not only our best tool, it is our best metaphor. It expands, it destroys because it broadens—as our thought broadens! A man's brain is a bomb! It must expand, even if it breaks up the universe!

MARQUIS
I don't want the universe broken up just yet. I want to do a lot of beastly things before I die. I thought of one just yesterday in bed...

SECRETARY
We're wandering away from the point, gentlemen. The only question is how Wednesday is to strike the blow. We should all agree with the original notion of a bomb. As to the actual arrangements, I suggest that tomorrow morning he should go to—

SUNDAY
(raising his hand, still facing away) —hold.

(The SECRETARY cuts herself off. The sound of a distant violin can be heard. It will play throughout)

SUNDAY
Again. Again! You hear him? That fellow with the violin, every day without fail. We fight the oppressors of this man, those who have left him no further choice but to beg for scraps with his remarkable talent. *(Beat. He listens)* Although, do

you know? For all his talent he seems to play only the same three songs, and I would wage a hundred wars just to free myself from such tyranny! I tell you, it is the contradiction of our lot. *(He turns back to the table)* Still. One can't help but admire his dedication. Were that sort to be found among our number, we could have toppled England by now. *(Beat)* We will speak no further of our plans at this moment.

GOGOL
(rising, incensed) Zso! Zso! Zis is how it is in zis land! You zay you nod 'ide, but it is nuzzinks! Ven at last ve talk importance, you zhut your mouth!

SUNDAY
Gogol, the most important ideas in the world are often those which remain unsaid. You seem to know nothing of mankind.

GOGOL
(with indignation) I die for zem and I slay zare oppressors!

SUNDAY
(standing) I see, I see. You die for mankind first, and then you get up and smite their oppressors. So that's all right.

GOGOL
Enough of this goncealment! I would zmite the tyrant in ze open square!

SUNDAY
Please control your beautiful sentiments and sit with your comrades at the table. For the first time this morning something intelligent is going to be said.

GOGOL
(hesitates, and then sits, muttering) Insufferable gombromise…

SUNDAY
I think. *(He walks around the table)* I think this has been spun out long enough. We grow complacent. Just now we were about to discuss plans and name places. I propose, before saying anything else that those plans and places are not to be voted upon at this meeting, but should instead be entrusted to the control of one reliable member. I suggest Comrade Saturday, Dr. Bull.

(The group seems shocked. At once, excepting SYME, they begin to speak. SUNDAY strikes the table forcefully)

SUNDAY
Not one. More word. At this table. Not one more tiny detail.

SECRETARY
Mr. President, this is highly irregular…

SUNDAY
Spare your regularity for your bowels. Think but a moment, and you will understand that only one thing could restrict our conversation here.

(Everyone seems to grasp it at once, with great shock. SYME makes subtle movements towards his pistol and stick. SUNDAY is standing very near him at this point)

SECRETARY
(standing, practically shrieking) It can't be! There can't—!

SUNDAY
There can and there is. We have a spy at this table.
I will waste no more words. *(Beat)* His name is
Gogol. He's that hairy humbug over there who
pretends to be a Pole.

*(GOGOL stands quickly, pushing his chair back,
brandishing a pistol in each hand)*

GOGOL
Aha! Now who is not good at deception!

*(The MARQUIS jumps up, twists GOGOL'S
arm behind his back, and places his dagger at
his throat. At the same time, DR. BULL grabs
GOGOL'S other wrist and pinches it, causing
him to drop his second pistol. DR. BULL has done
this without leaving his seat, and in fact, while
barely even looking at GOGOL. DE WORMS
has risen, slightly)*

MARQUIS
(speaking viciously into GOGOL'S ear) Enough
goncealment, hm? We shall see your entrails,
perhaps, when they are not goncealed under your
skin, your heart, your...

SUNDAY
SIT! DOWN!

*(A silence, save for the sound of the violin playing
in the distance. DE WORMS, the MARQUIS and
SECRETARY sit down. After a moment of confusion, so does GOGOL)*

SUNDAY
Now. Tragic child of Poland, might I inquire
under whose authority you infiltrate our circle?

GOGOL

(speaking now in a natural Cockney) Right-o. Game's up, I s'pose. With warm regards from Scotland Yard. *(He removes a small blue card from his waistcoat pocket and drops it on the table)*

SUNDAY

You understand the position you're now in.

GOGOL

(rising, stiffly, as if facing a firing squad) You bet. I see it's a fair cop. All I say is, I don't believe any Pole could have imitated my accent the way I imitated his.

SUNDAY

Inimitable, yes. I shall practice it in my bath. Do you mind leaving your beard behind with your credentials?

GOGOL

(removes his beard and drops it on the table) Not a bit. It was hot.

SUNDAY

You seemed to have kept pretty cool underneath it. *(Beat)* Now listen to me. I like you. The consequence of that is that it would annoy me for about two and a half minutes to hear you had died in agony. So understand…if you are ever to report to the police or any human soul the truth about us, I will endure that brief discomfort. On your discomfort I will not dwell. *(Beat)* Good day.

(A confused silence, save for the distant violin music. GOGOL steps past the other anarchists, nervously, and exits. SUNDAY returns to his chair,

but does not sit)

MARQUIS
You should have let us eviscerate him.

SUNDAY
A man is less useful eviscerated, my good Wednesday, than he is under threat of evisceration. You would have learned such by now, were your steel not so swift and brutal.

MARQUIS
Bah.

SUNDAY
Time is flying. I must go off at once; I have to take the chair at a Humanitarians meeting.

SECRETARY
Would it not be better if we were to discuss our plans first? Now that the spy has gone?

SUNDAY
I think not. Let Saturday settle it. I must be off; breakfast here in one week.

SECRETARY
(standing) It is a fundamental rule of our society that all plans be debated in full council! Now that the traitor is gone, would it not be more useful for us all—!

SUNDAY
Comrade Secretary, it might be useful if you went home and boiled your head for a turnip. I can't say. But it might. *(To the group)* It might also be useful if I weren't the only one watching out for spies! In one week, I expect this world to be lighter one Czar and one French President.

If that is not the case, I will have questions that none of you will be able to answer to my satisfaction. Good day.

(SUNDAY exits. One by one, grumbling slightly, the others stand and exit, leaving SYME alone in his chair)

END ACT II, SCENE ONE

Scene Two

(Immediately following the end of the previous scene. Members of the ENSEMBLE remove the table and chairs, and ultimately the railing. The stage goes dark save for a spotlight on SYME. The distant violin continues to play. He collects the small blue card left behind by GOGOL, removes his own blue card from his waistcoat, and compares the two, quietly.

After a moment of this, another spotlight appears onstage, nearby. DE WORMS stands in the light, staring at SYME intently. SYME becomes aware of DE WORMS; he stands, nervously, and walks out of the light. Light disappears on both the chair and DE WORMS. Spotlight appears on another chair, or bench, elsewhere onstage. SYME sits down and pulls both cards from his waistcoat again.

After a moment, DE WORMS once again appears in a nearby spotlight, staring intently at SYME.

This process occurs a number of times, with SYME growing increasingly disturbed as DE WORMS pursues him around the stage, or possibly around the entire theater.

Finally, SYME finds a seat at a wooden tavern table lit only by a small candle. The violin has faded away. He summons a WAITER and mutely orders a drink. He looks around the room, worried. Soon, he breathes easier.

At that moment, DE WORMS has a seat at the table across from SYME. He summons the WAITER and mutely orders a drink. He still stares at SYME with the same peering gaze. SYME looks back at him with curiosity.

The drinks arrive—a glass of scotch for SYME, a cup of tea for DE WORMS. SYME sips his scotch, DE WORMS simply stares)

SYME
My esteemed Professor. What an unexpected pleasure to meet you here. Was that you behind me all this afternoon? I confess that I saw you, but was unsure from the distance...*(Beat)* Truth be told, I wondered if it was some sort of initiation ritual that I had simply not been informed of earlier. "Perhaps," I thought, "the new Thursday is always chased along Cheapside, much as the new Lord Mayor is escorted along it." And might I add, comrade, that I, and I am sure many others, highly underestimate your constitution? *(Beat)* I was hoping that I would at some point be allowed to share a conversation with you. I have heard excellent things about you, Professor...the Nihilist of Nuremberg! You may only imagine my surprise—

although in hindsight it was obvious—to discover that you are our Friday.

(Pause. SYME downs his scotch)

SYME
(plainly) How may I help you, Professor?

DE WORMS
Are you a policeman?

SYME
A policeman? What could possess you to ask such a thing?

DE WORMS
The process was simple enough. I thought you looked like a policeman. I think so now.

SYME
Have I unknowingly put on a policeman's hat? Is there a number on me somewhere? Why must I be a policeman, comrade? Do let me be a postman, if I must be something. *(Beat)* But perhaps I misunderstand the delicacies of your German philosophy. Do you use policeman as a relative term? Do you say that any man may be a policeman, so that the gradient of possibility causes reality to have an imperceptible shade? If you say that a policeman may be the conclusion of a Gabriel Syme, and that all conclusions therefore exist simultaneously, then I can at last comprehend why you would think me a policeman. *(Beat)* In that case, I don't mind at all being a policeman. Frankly, I don't mind being anything in German.

DE WORMS
Are you on the police force? Are you a detective?

SYME

Your suggestion is ridiculous. I would even say it were insulting, were I not so amused by it. Why on earth would—?

DE WORMS

(sharply) —did you hear me ask a plain question, you paltering spy? Are you, or are you not, a police detective?

SYME

No!

DE WORMS

You swear it? You swear it? If you swear falsely, you will be damned! The devil will dance at your funeral! There is no mistake? You are an anarchist and a dynamiter? Above all, you are not in any sense in the British police?

SYME

(after a brief pause) I am not.

DE WORMS

That's a pity. *(He grabs SYME'S wrist with astonishing strength, his voice and demeanor changing to that of a much younger Englishman)* Because I am.

SYME

You're what? You're what?!

DE WORMS

(removes a blue card from his waistcoat) Scotland Yard. Anarchist Detail. Although, as you think policeman to be a relative term, I doubt the distinction means much to you. I thought I had been pursuing another lawman, and it turns out you're just another bloody dynamiter. I ought to arrest you out of spite if nothing else.

SYME
(grinning madly) Is that so? After this wretched
hour with you at my heels, my heart fit to burst?
You would claim spite? *(He pulls his blue card
from his waistcoat and lays it on the table)* I call!
Let us split the pot and arrest each other. *(He
begins to laugh, raucously, building to uncontrol-
lable)*

DE WORMS
(lets go of SYME'S wrist) Of all the bloody...
(comparing his own card to SYME'S)...pull yourself together, man. Have another drink. I'll join
you.

*(DE WORMS dumps the tea and snaps for the
WAITER, who instantly brings him something
much stiffer. SYME watches this with curiosity)*

SYME
You're not an old man at all, are you.

DE WORMS
That's not for me to say. For your assessment,
however: I was thirty-eight last birthday.

SYME
I mean...you're in perfect health. You have a grip
like a Greek wrestler. There's nothing the matter
with you.

DE WORMS
I am susceptible to colds.

SYME
(admiring the makeup) It's a remarkable job. Much
better than Gogol's. Even at the start I thought he
was a bit too hairy.

DE WORMS
It's a difference of artistic theory, Mr. Syme. Gogol, I suspect, is a romantic—he made himself up as a platonic abstract of an anarchist. I'm a realist, a portrait painter. More accurately, I am a portrait.

SYME
I have heard tell of the Professor de Worms for years now. All this time it's been you?

DE WORMS
Goodness no. The real Professor de Worms is, as I recall, currently living out his retirement in Naples.

SYME
Surely he knows about you?

DE WORMS
He does.

SYME
Then why hasn't he denounced you?

DE WORMS
Because I took the prodigiously clever step, if I may say so, of denouncing him first.

(*A NIHILIST, dressed to resemble DE WORMS, enters from one side of the stage in an isolated light, with a few members of the ENSEMBLE around him. DE WORMS stands and walks near the NIHILIST, continuing to narrate to SYME*)

DE WORMS
I approached him in a parlor in Berlin, in full view of his students, and I proclaimed that he could not be the celebrated Professor de Worms, as I was he. Oh, he tried to prove otherwise. He

attempted to counter me intellectually. He would say, for example, something that nobody but him could possibly understand.

NIHILIST
You are only De Worms in the manner of animals evolving into men. You lack the essential understanding of negation that allows you to differentiate between your eugenic identity and that of another.

DE WORMS
Obviously, I would counter with something not even I could understand. *(To NIHILIST)* "The principle of evolution is only negation, and the notion that involution functioned eugenically was long ago exposed by Pinckwerts and Glumpe."

SYME
Who?

DE WORMS
(to SYME) Devil if I know.

(The ENSEMBLE forcibly pulls NIHILIST offstage. The isolated light disappears, and DE WORMS returns to SYME)

DE WORMS
By the time I was done they were hounding him down the street. Awfully useful bit about nihilists: Since the only thing they believe in is nothing, it's not hard to make them believe anything. *(Beat)* It's a credit to the force that the two of us got this far.

SYME
Three of us. *(Beat. He removes the other blue card*

from his pocket and adds it to the pile on the table)
Although it is hardly to our credit that none of us
were aware of that.

DE WORMS
So you didn't know beforehand.

SYME
Nor you.

DE WORMS
I thought Sunday had nabbed me. I had my hand
on my revolver the whole time.

SYME
As did I.

DE WORMS
As did Gogol, evidently.

(Pause. They both sip their drinks)

SYME
(striking the table, suddenly) Damn and blast!
Three of us there! Three out of seven is a fighting
number! If only we had known we were three!

DE WORMS
It would not have been enough.

SYME
Three against four! And you only thirty-eight! It
would have been enough.

DE WORMS
Three against four, maybe. But not three against
Sunday.

SYME
Really, Professor, this is intolerable. Are you afraid
of this man?

DE WORMS
Yes I am. So are you.

(Pause. SYME has no retort)

SYME
Yes. I admit. I am. Therefore, by God, I must seek this man out and strike him on the mouth. Why, if heaven were his throne and the earth his footstool, I swear that I would bring him down. No man should leave anything in the universe of which he is afraid. *(He downs his drink, stands, and puts his hat on)* As the robber said on his deathbed: Thumb on the blade, and strike upwards.

DE WORMS
Where are you going?

SYME
I am going to stop this bomb being thrown in Paris.

(SYME strides off, purposefully. DE WORMS is left alone, nursing his drink. A moment later, SYME comes back and sits)

SYME
I have no idea how to do that.

DE WORMS
Indeed. If you recall, the plans for this affair were left entirely in the hands of the Marquis and Dr. Bull. The Marquis is likely on his way across the Channel already. This leaves us with Dr. Bull.

SYME
Do you know where to find him?

DE WORMS
From all I hear he wanders the streets at night
like some kind of bloody ghoul. He is a solitary
individual. He prefers his own company to that
of others, and I would not be in error to suggest
that the feeling is mutual.

SYME
There's something very wrong with him, isn't
there. He seems hollow inside.

(DR. BULL appears in an isolated light, frozen.
He grins placidly underneath his black spectacles)

DE WORMS
An apt description, yes. Most of the anarchists I
have met extol at length about the virtues of nihilism; Dr. Bull is nihilism. He has made a point of
knowing that oblivion to an extent not intended
for man. In his way, he is more terrifying than
Sunday. Sunday as a man is the embodiment of the
explosion; the fire and chaos and loud death. But
Dr. Bull...he is the quiet afterwards, when existence has ceased. When the universe ends, it will
sound like the soul of our Saturday.

(Pause. The isolated light vanishes)

SYME
You've spoken with him extensively.

DE WORMS
I was once at a pub with him and the Secretary.
It was...unpleasant.

SYME
(standing) Pleasant or not, we must make him
speak. If this plan succeeds...if Russia and France
are brought low...

DE WORMS
Then the rest of Europe may surely follow, yes.
Catastrophe.

SYME
Will you join me in the hunt?

DE WORMS
(standing, hesitant) I do not imagine I was
recruited for my cowardice, Mr. Syme. Indeed, if
I knew at all what my superior looked like, I'm
sure the expression on his face would be most
humbling if he found I did not accompany you.

SYME
You were recruited by an unseen man—

DE WORMS
—in a darkened room. You as well?

SYME
Yes. And now I would guess that Gogol experi-
enced the same. It seems the mode of our kind to
operate in the darkness.

(They exit. Blackout)

END ACT II, SCENE TWO

SCENE THREE

(The Vauxhall Bridge over the Thames River. Later evening, heavy fog, with peripheral glow of street lamps. DR. BULL stands on one side of the stage, staring seemingly straight ahead into space over the guard wall. He is almost perfectly still.

A CONSTABLE strolls past him, takes notice, and stops. They stand next to DR. BULL and attempt to see what he is staring at)

CONSTABLE
Evening. Nice night, wot?

(DR. BULL acknowledges CONSTABLE with the slightest of nods. He does not look at them)

CONSTABLE
(peering into the distance) River's quiet. I like that. *(Beat)* What's that you're lookin' at, then?

(DR. BULL turns slowly to face CONSTABLE. He smiles disconcertingly)

DR. BULL
Nothing at all. What is it you're looking at.

(The CONSTABLE seems shaken to their core. They take a step back, nervously)

CONSTABLE
Evening, then.

(They walk away across the stage, cautiously but not in any hurry. DR. BULL resumes his staring, the smile still on his face. As CONSTABLE walks offstage, SYME and DE WORMS walk on and stop as they see DR. BULL. They speak in stage whispers)

DE WORMS
There. I should take the lead, I've had more experience dealing with Dr. Bull than you.

SYME
Agreed. *(Beat)* We should have specific word-signals, I think, to let the other know if things are going poorly.

DE WORMS
Word-signals?

SYME
If you were to utter the word "coeval," for example, I would know you needed some sort of assistance.

DE WORMS
"Coeval"?

SYME
Or "lush." I've always rather fancied the word "lush."

DE WORMS
(irritated) Under what possible circumstances do you suppose I would use the word "lush" in this conversation?

SYME
Speak of grass. Speak of the way petty tyrants forced their subjects to eat lush, green grass...

DE WORMS
Good God, man, don't you realize this is serious?

SYME
I'm aware it's serious. It's more than serious; it's tragedy. Always be comic in tragedy, I say. Find the comedy in tragedy and there you shall find the truth.

DE WORMS
You sound like some sort of bloody poet, Syme.

SYME
I am some sort of bloody poet, Professor.

DE WORMS
Magnificent. Let's find out if that's good for anything.

(DE WORMS re-affects his feeble German manner. They walk across the stage and place themselves on either side of DR. BULL. If he notices either of them he makes little sign of it)

DE WORMS
Well met, comrade. Don't turn your head. *(Beat)* You've made all of the arrangements for the Paris affair, I take it?

(Pause. DR. BULL gives the slightest of nods)

DE WORMS
I apologize if I am abrupt; I only hope we are not
too late. We have information, Dr. Bull, which
we must give you without delay. (Beat) Comrade
Syme and I have had an alarming experience this
evening. It would take too much time to recount
it, but we must urge you to alter what plans you
have set, or if those plans are already in motion,
to follow our agent with all speed. The operation
is in grave jeopardy.

DR. BULL
Jeopardy.

DE WORMS
Yes.

DR. BULL
You would agree that the very nature of our
operations is to be in jeopardy. Yes. Our plans
in constant threat of being foiled. You would
agree.

DE WORMS
I...suppose so, comrade, but...

DR. BULL
Then it would seem that the operation is proceed-
ing as expected.

DE WORMS
I'm afraid you don't understand.

DR. BULL
How strange that my lack of understanding should
frighten you.

DE WORMS
Dr. Bull. Please. I speak to you with great sever-

ity. Our experience this evening…it was…I assure you…

SYME
(interjecting) Here I should take up the narrative, I think, as the encounter was mine. I had the extraordinary good fortune, you see, of falling into conversation with a police detective earlier this evening. The man was intoxicated, and a right boastful sort—I will spare you an imitation, but suffice to say that Scotland Yard has uncovered the Marquis, and intends to arrest him the moment he sets foot in Paris.

DE WORMS
Syme came to me immediately with this information. It seemed to me to be unquestionably urgent.

SYME
Unless we get on his track, Doctor, all will be lost.

(Pause. DR. BULL, apparently lost in thought, walks a few feet away from the other two)

DR. BULL
A dilemma. Yes. A dilemma indeed. And the question remains as how to resolve it.

DE WORMS
We've already told you what's to be done—!

DR. BULL
—not. That. No. *(He turns on the two men and draws a pistol on them)* The dilemma of what is to be done with the two of you.

(DE WORMS and SYME raise their hands)

DE WORMS
Dr. Bull, have you lost your senses?!

DR. BULL
Instructions were given. You see. Instructions
given by our Sunday. "Dr. Bull," he says, "most
important. Kill any man, woman, or child who
may approach you in regards to the Paris conspiracy." Very clear instructions.

DE WORMS
Surely he didn't mean us!

DR. BULL
I would not say that I know the mind of Sunday.
I would not say that you know the mind of
Sunday. Sooner a man know the mind of a
mountain than a man know the mind of that
mountain of a man.

DE WORMS
What?

DR. BULL
A dilemma. A quandary. I am meant to take
Sunday either at his word or at his intention. If
one assumes. That is. Assumes that his word and
intention are dissimilar in this instance. *(Beat)*
Yes. The assumption informs the dilemma. The
assumption is that you are particularly excluded
from Sunday's edict. If there is to be no distinction between members of the Council and the
general population, then the instruction is without ambiguity. There is no Comrade Thursday.
There is no Comrade Friday. There are only two
men. As these men have approached myself the
Dr. Bull on the matter of the Paris affair and have

no qualifying status, it would seem prudent to shoot the both of them now. *(He takes aim)*

DE WORMS
No! Wait!

DR. BULL
But there is then the question of regards. "In regards to the Paris conspiracy." The question of the information presented. One may contend that the information is not in regards to the Paris conspiracy, per se, but rather in regards to Scotland Yard's conspiracy to thwart the Paris conspiracy. One may contend. In as such as the information does not fit the criteria of the directive, then it would be an error to kill you. *(He pulls the pistol back)*

(DE WORMS and SYME slowly lower their hands)

DE WORMS
I am glad you see reason, Dr. Bull...

(DR. BULL points the pistol at them again. DE WORMS and SYME raise their hands again)

DR. BULL
"See" reason. No. One does not "see" reason, Professor. Reason is, after all, insensible. *(Beat)* Perspective. You see. Yes. Your reason is not my reason. Within your reason it is absurd to be killed and it is absurd for me to kill you. Within my reason it is reasonable to kill you. Even if killing you would be absurd it would be within my reason. I may kill you for no reason at all. I may kill you within all reason. You may reason with me to be reasonable and in being reasonable I may kill you. *(As he continues this monologue, he*

begins to lose attention of the other two men, and pace slightly) It is reasonable to believe that the reason for living is to die. Yes. As no living thing fails to die, it would be unreasonable to think that there is any other reason to live than to die. Born to oblivion. Yes. The essence of anarchy. To tear down those institutions that purport control over an existence controlled only by chaos. The aim of the anarchist. To vault society ever closer to the pure void at the end of all things. The world rots until there is no time of any kind. No numbers save zero. *(Beat. He is turned away from the two men, some distance away, lost in thought, the pistol at his side)* Yes.

(Pause. SYME whispers cautiously to DE WORMS)

SYME
What exactly is Dr. Bull a doctor of, Professor?

DE WORMS
I never thought to ask, you know that?

(The two make an attempt to sneak up on DR. BULL. He stops them with a swift raise of his pistol, still turned away from them. They raise their hands again)

DR. BULL
No time of any kind. Certainly no Thursdays or Fridays. *(He turns to them)* In which case neither the word nor the intention of Sunday has any meaning. Step back, comrades.

(They do so)

DE WORMS
This is insanity, Dr. Bull. While you philosophize and threaten us, you ignore the very real danger

that we have been trying to warn you of. The Marquis—!

DR. BULL
—yes. The Marquis. The Marquis must be alerted.

DE WORMS
If this is finished, then—

DR. BULL
—the awareness of the Marquis and your deaths are exclusive entities. You would agree.

DE WORMS
I give up. What use is reason against madmen? Go ahead, shoot us, at least we'll be shut of this nonsense. Syme, if you have anything to say? Coeval, then. Lush.

SYME
(after a short moment) I confess, Dr. Bull—if I'm to die here, you do have my gratitude.

DE WORMS
Gratitude?

DR. BULL
Unexpected. Explain, Comrade Thursday.

SYME
I mean nothing byzantine by it. Only that I find it poetic to be cast into the void by one who understands it as well as you do.

DE WORMS
Syme, what are you doing?

SYME
I told you, Professor. I seek the comedy.

DE WORMS
Then you shall die laughing.

SYME
I do not know that I shall die at all. Look past the end of the firearm, my friend. *(He takes a tentative step forward, arms still raised, and speaks directly and enthusiastically to DR. BULL)* Look at the ingenious aesthetics of you. The hat, the coat, the infernal goggles, the language games, the impossible devotion to oblivion—all by which you made certain nobody dared to see you at all. But is a true nihilist the product of so much effort? I think not. *(To DE WORMS)* This man is no nihilist; this man is a nightmare. He is a thing sculpted of one's worst fears of anarchy, and to whose worst fears belong the anarchist?

DE WORMS
The state.

SYME
The state! *(He removes his blue card from his pocket)* Dr. Bull, would you happen to be a policeman? The Professor and I are.

DE WORMS
Syme! *(He looks from SYME to DR. BULL, sighs, then removes his own card from his pocket and holds it up alongside SYME'S)* Poets.

(Pause. DR. BULL removes his glasses. SYME lowers his hands as the two look into each other's faces. DR. BULL embraces SYME with a profound sense of relief. His voice and demeanor is suddenly young and vibrant)

DR. BULL
I'm awfully glad you chaps came when you did.

SYME
Fancy that. I'm a better poet than I thought.

DR. BULL
(holds up his own blue card) Anarchist Detail.
Yourselves?

SYME
The same. Good show, detective.

DR. BULL
As yourself, sir.

DE WORMS
Lord God Almighty. If this is true, then there
were more detectives on that damned council
than there were dynamiters!

DR. BULL
Neither of you knew of Gogol?

SYME
Nor each other until a few hours ago. I take it you
were recruited much the same way we were…

DR. BULL
Shady bloke in the darkened room?

DE WORMS
That's the one. *(Beat)* It's all some bloody game,
isn't it?

DR. BULL
Could be. Haven't the foggiest who's playing at it,
now. I told him, when he pulled me in, that I didn't
know the first thing about this sort of business.
I'm just a poor mathematics student, I told him.

I can't go about infiltrating any Central Anarchist Council. I asked him the same thing you just asked: What use is reason against madmen, I asked.

DE WORMS
To which he replied?

DR. BULL
He didn't. *(Beat)* He tossed these spectacles at my feet and didn't say one word more.

SYME
You seem to have done all right, detective. Truth be told, you and your spectacles were our greatest terror on the council.

DR. BULL
Is that so? I daresay you've underestimated the Marquis.

(The MARQUIS appears in a spotlight, frozen, toying with his dagger)

DE WORMS
(bitterly) Are we sure he's not a detective as well? We seem to have shaken quite a few from the tree as of late.

SYME
To think we were four against three...

DE WORMS
Four against one. Four against Sunday. Unless the Marquis is also...

DR. BULL
There's no mistake on this one. The Marquis' a villain. You know of the attack on the Piccadilly courthouse, I'm sure. The assassination of Lord Wainwright.

DE WORMS
Those were him?

DR. BULL
As I know for certain. Might be others I can't prove yet. I've made a study of him, I have, and believe me when I tell you: There's no compassion in that man, not for those he's killed nor for anyone else. Those he doesn't slaughter with dynamite he murders in senseless duels.

DE WORMS
I would remind you, sir, that you very nearly shot both of us not moments ago.

DR. BULL
True. But at the time I was sure that the two of you were anarchists. The Marquis will not discriminate. No compassion, and certainly no law.

(The spotlight disappears on the MARQUIS)

SYME
Well, that's a relief. *(Beat)* That is, it will be a welcome change of pace to oppose an actual fiend instead of all these invented ones. I take it that you were set to thwart him yourself before we arrived?

DR. BULL
It would have been ideal to give him a faulty arrangement, but I feared his suspicion.

DE WORMS
Will we still be able to catch him?

DR. BULL
I've timed it all. He'll still be at Calais when we arrive. There's a steam-ship coming down the

river as we speak; it will take us to another boat near the Channel. Mind you, I hadn't formed a plan to stop the Marquis once I arrived at Calais, but perhaps with the two of you... *(He looks over the railing)* There it is now. We should be off.

(DE WORMS and DR. BULL exit, leaving SYME looking towards the oncoming boat. He seems to be thinking intently. Finally, he smiles and follows the two offstage)

SYME
Duels, you said?

(SYME exits. Lights fade out)

END ACT II

ACT III

SCENE ONE

(A café in Calais, mid-afternoon. There is the distant sound of a brass band playing a Wagner composition.

The MARQUIS sits at a table with a French COLONEL and LIEUTENANT. The three men are playing a casual game of cards)

MARQUIS
There is an art to it, mes amís. An art to politics. In fact, it is the only true art that a gentleman need concern himself with.

LIEUTENANT
A bold statement, m'sieu Marquis. You do not believe a gentleman should paint, then?

COLONEL
Or sculpt?

LIEUTENANT
(to the COLONEL, competitively) Poetry!

COLONEL
Opera!

LIEUTENANT
Le cuisine.

COLONEL
L'amour.

LIEUTENANT
(conceding) Oui.

COLONEL
All gentlemanly pursuits, Marquis.

MARQUIS
Simple crafts, next to politics. Ink, or stone, or the thighs of whores, how can it feel to handle such trifles after your hands have shaped society itself?

LIEUTENANT
You might be surprised, if you know whom to ask for.

COLONEL
As if you were one to speak on politics, m'sieu... you with your life of leisure. I doubt you even know who France's president is. I doubt you know any more about politics than you know about this card game.

MARQUIS
Perhaps not. But I never claimed to be a gentleman.

(He lays down his cards; a winning hand. The COLONEL and LIEUTENANT look at his cards in disbelief. The LIEUTENANT takes the cards back and reshuffles them)

(SYME walks onstage towards the café table, slowly, seeming to be drunk. As he gets closer to the MARQUIS, he stops, slowly recognizing him. The MARQUIS takes notice of SYME and views him with parts confusion, disgust, and amusement)

SYME
The Marquis de St. Eustache, I believe.

MARQUIS
The celebrated Mr. Syme, I presume. What a surprise to see you in Calais. How are you?

SYME
Oh...*(He switches to an exaggerated Cockney)*... just the Syme. *(Giggles drunkenly)* Permit me to pull your nose. *(He makes a wild grab for the MARQUIS' nose)*

MARQUIS
(jumping back) The devil—?!

(SYME makes another grab for the MARQUIS' nose; the COLONEL and LIEUTENANT stand and restrain SYME)

COLONEL
Enough of that...

LIEUTENANT
Ill-mannered...

COLONEL
Perhaps would be best if you...

SYME
(pointing at the MARQUIS and declaiming loudly to the café) This man has insulted me!

LIEUTENANT
Insulted you? When?

SYME
Just now! He insulted my mother.

LIEUTENANT
Insulted your mother?

SYME
Well, anyhow…my aunt.

COLONEL
Impossible. How can the Marquis have insulted your mother—

SYME
—aunt!—

COLONEL
—aunt, that is, how can he have insulted your aunt just now? He has been sitting here the whole time.

SYME
Ahhhh…it was what he said.

MARQUIS
I have said nothing of any sort about your mother—

SYME
—aunt!—

MARQUIS
—aunt, grandmother, cousin, or any other relation of yours. I have been conversing with these men on the nature of politics. I may have commented on the band; I do enjoy hearing Wagner played well.

SYME
That! That was it! That's the one. Wagner! An allusion to my family. My aunt played Wagner very badly and it remains a most painful subject. We are constantly insulted about it.

LIEUTENANT
Come now, man, I am sure that the Marquis meant no such—

SYME
—I assure you...your conversation was packed to the gills with references to my aunt's weaknesses.

COLONEL
Nonsense! I have barely said anything for half an hour; save that I liked the singing of that girl with the black hair.

SYME
There you are again! My aunt's hair was red!

COLONEL
It seems to me that you are simply seeking a pretext to insult the Marquis.

SYME
By! George! What a clever chap you are!

(He lunges again at the MARQUIS' nose. The MARQUIS dodges back, but SYME manages to grab his shirt and tear a small opening in it)

MARQUIS
Peste! You're as drunk as an owl!

SYME
Better drunk as an owl than as ugly as a rhinoceros!

MARQUIS
(furious) So be it! Seeking a quarrel with me, Syme? Mon dieu, there was never a man who had to seek long. *(He removes a glove from his pocket and slaps SYME across the face with it)* There are still four hours of daylight left. Find yourself a second and let us fight this evening.

SYME
(straightening himself up and smoothing his clothes, but still drunkenly) Marquis. Your action is worthy of your fame and your blood. However, I would wonder what it would do for your reputation if we met this evening and you so quickly dispatched an opponent who only a few hours earlier had barely been able to stand. I propose a delay. Tomorrow morning, shortly after seven?

MARQUIS
You dare dictate conditions! You are fortunate I do not kill you where you stand, drunk or no!

SYME
Then I thank the Marquis for my good fortune, and humbly request again. Let us settle this tomorrow morning, shortly after seven.

MARQUIS
Seven. I...that is...

COLONEL
(to the MARQUIS) Come, m'sieu, it is only proper to allow this small concession.

MARQUIS
There is an appointment...I do not...

LIEUTENANT
(to the MARQUIS) He is right. An uncouth fool, but he is right: there is no honor in dueling a disabled foe. Leave it until the morning.

MARQUIS
But you do not understand, it is vital that...

COLONEL
Marquis.

MARQUIS
(hesitant, but resigned) Tomorrow morning at seven. *(Beat)* But I shall choose the location. Surely I can be allowed that in return.

COLONEL
It is only fair.

MARQUIS
There is a meadow...near the railway station. Steel?

SYME
As you wish.

MARQUIS
I do. *(He steps to SYME and hisses in his face)* If you are not there, I will find you, Syme. I care not where you sit at our table. Tomorrow your death will be swift, beyond tomorrow it will be less so.

SYME
(brightly) Why...how true that is, Marquis!

(The MARQUIS turns on his heel and strides off. The COLONEL and LIEUTENANT follow. SYME watches them go. After a moment, he composes himself—he is completely sober. He has a seat and lets out a profound sigh of relief. DE WORMS and

DR. BULL *walk onstage and approach SYME)*

DE WORMS
That was sport, Syme.

SYME
You insult me, Professor. That…was art. *(Beat)* I have done it. I have fixed a fight on the beast, for seven tomorrow. This gives me a chance to prevent him from catching the 7:30 train to Paris—if he misses that, he misses his crime?

DR. BULL
Yes. There would be no other opportunity.

SYME
He has selected that small meadow near the railway station as our battlefield. He will trust in killing me in time to catch the train. But I am no poor fencer myself, and I think I can keep him in play, at any rate, until the train is lost. *(Beat)* Then perhaps he may kill me to console his feelings.

DR. BULL
And we shall be your seconds for this duel?

SYME
If you would.

DE WORMS
Of course, but I wonder what the Marquis will make of it, to see half the Council up in arms against him.

DR. BULL
Perhaps he will think it some test designed by Sunday.

SYME
Has he done such a thing before?

DE WORMS
No. But he could. *(Beat)* The core of Sunday's power is in what he might do, not in what he does.

SYME
Professor, forgive me, but any more of your dark bugbears about Sunday's immeasurable powers and I will become positively ill. He is a man, no demon. His reach is no more than the length of his shoulder to his hand, and beyond that he must go to creatures like the Marquis to exercise his will. What Sunday might do? *(He stands)* What we might do is preserve the lives of no lesser men than the Czar and the President of France! What we might do is thwart such nefarious plots against civilization, what we might do is stand steadfast as the watchmen on the wall of humanity itself!

(Pause. The brass band, in the distance, has built to a crescendo)

DE WORMS
We also might watch the Marquis run you through in a matter of seconds and be on his merry bomb-throwing way.

(The brass band stops, cacophonously)

SYME
Honestly, my friend. You've been a nihilist for far too long.

(He exits. DE WORMS and DR. BULL look at each other, shrug their shoulders, and follow him out)

END ACT III, SCENE ONE

Scene Two

(A clearing, near dawn. The shadows of tall trees fall upon the ground. The MARQUIS stands to one side, with the COLONEL and LIEUTENANT nearby, practicing forms with a rapier and dagger. SYME is nowhere to be seen)

MARQUIS
The time.

LIEUTENANT
(checking a watch) Ten after

MARQUIS
At quarter after, I declare his throat forfeit. *(He makes a vicious lunge with the dagger)*

COLONEL
I admit I am disappointed. He seemed an honorable sort, even for a drunken fool.

MARQUIS
The ti—

LIEUTENANT
—eleven after.

MARQUIS
What sort of man sets a time and refuses to keep it?
(He stops, and hands the sword to the COLONEL)
I have heard of lands in Asia where the practice of
torture has been honed to a master craft. At times
like these I lament my lack of travel.

*(SYME enters, followed by DE WORMS and DR.
BULL. The MARQUIS is facing away from them,
but notes the expression on the COLONEL'S and
LIEUTENANT'S faces. There is an awkward silence)*

SYME
Oh. *(Beat)* This meadow.

MARQUIS
(spins around, angrily) At last! I am going to—!
*(He is startled to notice DE WORMS and DR.
BULL, but quickly composes himself)* Friday.
Saturday.

DE WORMS and DR. BULL
Wednesday.

SYME
(bowing) And Thursday.

MARQUIS
But why are you…? When did you…? *(Beat)* Have
I done something to displease…? *(Beat)* You are
acting on Syme's behalf?

DE WORMS
We are.

MARQUIS
This is…most unexpected…

SYME
Indeed. *(Beat)* Seeing so many of us here almost
makes one weak, hm?

Pause. The MARQUIS seems hesitant.

LIEUTENANT
(looking at his watch) Quarter after.

MARQUIS
(snapping out of it) What are we waiting for? *(He
grabs his rapier from the COLONEL, roughly)* Let
us on with it.

*(DE WORMS, DR. BULL, the COLONEL and
the LIEUTENANT step to center stage)*

COLONEL
I suggest, on behalf of the Marquis de St. Eustache,
that these combatants should duel only to the
first considerable hurt.

DR. BULL
Unacceptable. Our comrade was insistent that the
duel be fought to the death.

COLONEL
To the death! That seems—

DR. BULL
—if the Marquis is not willing to—

DE WORMS
—gentlemen. Let us split the difference, and
agree that our fellows should play only until one
is disabled. It must be a matter of indifference
which method is adopted, and our principal has
strong reasons for demanding the longer encounter, reasons the delicacy of which prevent me
from being explicit—

LIEUTENANT
—fine, fine! Agreed!

(They return to their corners. SYME hands DE WORMS his hat and cloak. He stands holding his stick in front of him as the MARQUIS enters a dueling stance)

MARQUIS
Forget your weapon, comrade?

SYME
(drawing the sword from his stick) Hardly, my good man.

COLONEL
En garde. Engagez.

(They duel. The MARQUIS fights to end the combat quickly; SYME fights much more defensively, attacking when able but otherwise fencing with the intention of drawing out the combat. The MARQUIS may graze SYME, SYME may graze the MARQUIS. The duel should, for the first part of the fight, heavily favor the MARQUIS.

In the middle of the duel, a train whistle should be heard clearly in the distance. This will distract the MARQUIS momentarily, and SYME will take the opportunity, very nearly managing a killing stroke that the MARQUIS will only just manage to parry. From this point, the MARQUIS will attack with a fierce recklessness, which SYME will exploit to gain the upper hand, although he remains unable to land a considerable blow. The roar of the oncoming train grows closer and louder as they fight, culminating in a piercing whistle indicating that the train has arrived at its station. The MARQUIS *leaps away from the fight, tosses his weapons aside, and raises a hand to yield)*

MARQUIS
Stop! Stop! One moment.

COLONEL
Qu'est-ce qui c'est passe? Has there been foul play?

DE WORMS
None until now. Do you yield, Marquis?

MARQUIS
(in a state of mild panic) A trap. My God, a trap!

DE WORMS
Do you surrender, Marquis?

MARQUIS
A TRAP!

DR. BULL
(to SYME and DE WORMS) Aha. I think he's figured it out, then. *(to MARQUIS)* Right-o, Marquis, it is a trap. We are not your fellow anarchists, we are—

MARQUIS
(his French accent dropping, bit by bit, into an aristocratic English)—I know what you are! I know! Why are you here? To assist me? No, of course not, to stop me. Why else would you be here? And how do I know? *(He holds up a blue card)* Because it's exactly what I would do! *(He removes his nose)* Yesterday you asked for my nose, Syme. Here. *(He peels off his mustache)* Have the mustache as well, if you wish. *(He peels off his beard, at last revealing a woman beneath the disguise)* For that matter,

take all of this monstrosity off of me. God knows I'm only too glad to be rid of him!

LIEUTENANT
Mon dieu! Colonel, do you see...the Marquis, he is, ah, that is to say, she is...

SYME
(tossing his sword down, disgusted) Again! Again with this insufferable, blundering balderdash! This...

LIEUTENANT
...the Marquess? No, that is not...

DR. BULL
I don't believe it...

SYME
...God-forsaken, misguided, doddering...

MARQUIS
Do you understand, detectives?

SYME
...the whole bally lot of us!

LIEUTENANT
...Marquette?

COLONEL
(livid) Madame Marquise! This, this masquerade of yours, it is improper, it is insulting, is, is...

MARQUIS
My good colonel, I know, I know what you must think, but I promise you this is a mistake.

COLONEL
A mistake?! Do I not behold before me a woman daring to disguise herself as a man?

MARQUIS
Yes, you do, and that woman disguised as a man was also a man disguised as an assassin, while in truth all of us before you now are detectives of Scotland Yard—

DR. BULL
(stepping forward, fiercely)—I say I do not believe you, devil! Piccadilly! Lord Wainwright! Whosoever else's blood stains your hands…you would have us believe that these were the actions of an officer of the law?!

MARQUIS
Comrade Saturday, if I may continue to call you such; now is hardly the time to discuss matters of law enforcement method—

DR. BULL
—method?! Those were His Majesty's subjects you butchered! Detective or no, woman or no, I'll see you pay for—

MARQUIS
(exasperated)—do you have the slightest idea, you impertinent gosling, exactly how many hours each morning it takes to sculpt this Gallic brute around my body? To move my limbs and muscles with such delicate precision as to not have had the charade unravel while standing mere inches away from our mutual quarry?

DR. BULL
…no. But. The bombs.

MARQUIS
Then could you kindly understand that Piccadilly, that Lord Wainwright, that they were illusions

just as elaborate as the Marquis has been! I could explain them in detail, but now is not the time! Are you not listening to me? TRAP!

DE WORMS
As was our intention.

MARQUIS
Hell take your intentions, I am speaking of his, of Sunday's! Lieutenant! Are you still wont to carrying around opera glasses?

LIEUTENANT
(withdrawing them, sheepishly) Oui, m'sieu, ah, mademoiselle, but...

MARQUIS
(grabbing them and peering into the distance) There! Exactly as I feared. (Thrusting the glasses at SYME) See for yourself.

(Pause. SYME'S expression grows grim)

SYME
The Secretary.

DE WORMS
What? Here? Why?

MARQUIS
Gentlemen, we have been remarkably played.

SYME
What do you mean?

MARQUIS
Sunday! Can you not think of anything more Sunday than this, that he should put all of his powerful enemies on the Supreme Council, and then take care that it was not supreme?

DE WORMS
He's known the whole time! He gave Bull the assignment of planning so that we would pursue Bull, and then watched us all chase the Marquis to here...and here we all are now in a tidy package.

MARQUIS
Confounded babies playing blind man's bluff!

DE WORMS
Babies, yes. Less than that.

MARQUIS
Quite right. Killing the Supreme Council is a trivial matter, like a postcard...it may be left to his Secretary.

SYME
(peering through the opera glasses) The Secretary and that mob, you mean.

DR. BULL
(going to SYME'S side) Mob?

SYME
The one that just stepped off that train behind her.

(DR. BULL removes his spectacles, takes the opera glasses, and looks through them)

DE WORMS
It cannot be as bad as you say. There are a good number of them, certainly, but they may easily be ordinary tourists.

DR. BULL
Do ordinary tourists wear black masks halfway up the face?

(A sickened pause. DR. BULL hands the opera glasses back to the LIEUTENANT)

MARQUIS
Our time is short. I would urge that we escape at once, in our own separate ways, and find each other again in London. Agreed?

DE WORMS
Agreed.

SYME
Agreed.

DR. BULL
Agreed.

(Giving each other one last look, they rush off in separate directions, leaving the COLONEL and LIEUTENANT alone in the meadow, befuddled)

COLONEL
T'as compris quelque chose toi?

LIEUTENANT
Moins que toi, j'en suis certain.

COLONEL
Ces anglais...Ils sont...

LIEUTENANT
...fous?

COLONEL
Oui.

(The COLONEL and LIEUTENANT exit)

END ACT THREE, SCENE TWO

SCENE THREE

(The meadow, immediately following Scene Two. The SECRETARY walks slowly onstage with a self-satisfied smirk on her face. She holds her pocket watch in her hand and stares at it, as if waiting.

After a moment, SYME, DE WORMS, DR. BULL, and the MARQUIS are pushed forcibly onstage by members of the MOB, who are wearing black bandannas over the bottom half of their faces. The four detectives have had cloth bags placed over their heads. They are forced to their knees in the meadow. The SECRETARY puts her watch away)

SECRETARY
How pleasant at last for us all to know who we are and where we stand, eh? Or kneel, as the case may be. (Beat) You thought yourselves clever men, I take it. Clever men, masters of trickery, but We Have Known. Yes, we have known who you are for some time now. It must

be a disappointment to you to discover that.
Just as it must be a disappointment for you to
know how many of us there are. *(Beat)* Did you
think the world was your ally, little men? That
you outnumbered us? Ha. Ha! The world is not
what you would have it be, it is what we would
have it be. If you had only understood this.
If you had only understood, you would have
given up long ago, and would not find yourselves in your predicament. A pity, because you
are clever men. Clever and resourceful. But
unfortunate that, in spite of such qualities, you
simply lacked the ability to choose the correct
side. *(Beat)* Do you have anything to say for
yourselves? Hm? *(Beat)* To think that at the
last so many clever men would find themselves
struck dumb.

SYME
You want an epitaph, is that it? I'll give you
no such thing. *(He pushes himself to stand, but is
restrained by the MOB)* Know this, though. This
meadow we stand in? You did not create it. The
world you would claim as yours? It does not
belong to you. You do not make the lantern
and you do not light it, and it will be here long
after your empire of apes—! *(SYME rips himself
free of the MOB and tears the bag from his head)*
Your empire of apes has withered and its ashes
have fallen into the sea! "Anything to say for
ourselves!" I have something to say, yes I do
indeed—

SECRETARY
—enough of these lunatic ravings—

SYME
—and even in this lion's den I'll die with this last act of defiance roaring forth from this mouth, that you, *Madam Secretary*—

SECRETARY
—Dr. Bull. Professor de Worms. Marquis de St. Eustache. And you, *Mr. Gabriel Syme*—

SECRETARY AND SYME
(pointing at each other)—ARE UNDER ARREST IN THE NAME OF THE LAW!

Pause. Suddenly, DE WORMS, DR. BULL, and the MARQUIS release an ear-splitting scream of primal frustration.

DE WORMS
I know now! I do! I am in Bedlam!

DR. BULL
This isn't insanity, this is a nightmare!

MARQUIS
This is no nightmare, this is hell!

SECRETARY
Shut up, all of you! Shut up! You arrest me? How on earth can you...?

SYME
(sighs, removes his card from his pocket) Never mind. Detective.

(GOGOL removes his mask and speaks to the SECRETARY)

GOGOL
You said they were—!

SECRETARY
—I thought they were!

GOGOL
A lot of bloody flats we are.

SECRETARY
(to the MOB) Let them up.

(DE WORMS, DR. BULL, and the MARQUIS are helped to their feet, the bags removed from their heads. GOGOL and the SECRETARY may briefly register the truth about the MARQUIS but otherwise set that realization aside for now)

SECRETARY
But the Supreme Anarchist Council...

MARQUIS
What Supreme Anarchist Council?

DE WORMS
We're all stupid policemen looking at each other, that's all.

(Pause. They are all unsure what to do)

DR. BULL
Well. I don't know about the rest of you, but this stupid policeman could stand for a stiff drink. *(He walks off)* All who wish to join me are welcome.

MARQUIS
I second that. *(She exits)*

DE WORMS
Third. Anybody wishing the motion carried may follow me.

(DE WORMS exits with the MOB)

SECRETARY
But...but surely Sunday, at least, must be...

SYME
Who's to say anymore? We shall have to ask him when we next see him.

(SYME exits, leaving the SECRETARY in the meadow. Lights fade out)

END ACT THREE

ACT IV

Scene One

(The balcony of the café where the Supreme Council had previously met for breakfast. SUNDAY relaxes, reading a newspaper. A violin can be heard in the distance.

SYME, DE WORMS, DR. BULL, GOGOL, the MARQUIS and the SECRETARY walk on, purposefully. SUNDAY seems to not notice them. They surround him. He continues to read his newspaper. The SECRETARY clears her throat loudly)

SUNDAY
(lowering the paper) Delightful! So pleased to see you all! Are the Czar and President dead?

SECRETARY
(stiffly) No, sir. There has been no massacre.

SUNDAY
I don't recall asking for a massacre, Madam Secretary. Just a plain double assassination, that

was all I desired. You may massacre on your own time, if you wish, but my orders were not so grotesque.

SECRETARY
We have no time for this tomfoolery.

SUNDAY
Alas, there is never time for tomfoolery. It is the very waste of time that makes tomfoolery so precious.

SECRETARY
We have come to know what all of this means! Who are you? What are you? Why did you get us all here? How did you know who and what we are? Are you a half-witted man playing conspirator or a mastermind playing the fool? Answer me!

SUNDAY
(putting the paper down entirely) If I understand the thrust of your survey...you wish to know what I am, what you are, what my hat is, what the Council is, and what the world is. Well, I may go so far as to rend the veil of one mystery. If you want to know what you are; you are a set of highly well-intentioned young jackasses.

SYME
And you? What are you!

SUNDAY
I? What am I? Why should I be anything more than a riddle? Fix your eyes on what you know— you poets, you professors, you policemen—fix your eyes on the sea and the sky and the common criminals and understand those, for you won't ever understand me.

GOGOL
(drawing a pistol on SUNDAY) I couldn't give two quid if I understand him. All that matters to this one is that he's under arrest.

SUNDAY
(with a savage glee) ARREST me? How do you expect to contain me, wretched thing? You think I haven't been cornered such before; I have been hunted by better than you sorry bunch and here I still stand. Hunted since the beginning of time, hunted by kings and sages; all the churches and all the philosophers! You cannot arrest me until you know me, and you cannot know me until—

(SUNDAY stops mid-sentence and suddenly vaults over the back railing. The others are stunned. They rush to the railing and lean to look over. As soon as they do so, SUNDAY'S head pops back up. He had never let go of the railing)

SUNDAY
There's one thing I'll tell you, though, about who I am. I'm the man in the dark room, who made you all detectives.

(He lets go of the railing and drops for real. The others lean over the railing)

DE WORMS
You know, I was rather afraid he'd tell us something like that.

MARQUIS
(pointing) There the devil goes! After him!

(The detectives rush off the stage, and the violin begins a loud tarantella. What follows is a series of

"chase" sequences that span the stage and theater space. It begins with the six detectives running on to the center of the stage and realizing that they have lost SUNDAY. They split in half and run off in separate directions, criss-crossing the space, shouting desperately for him to stop, interrogating members of the ENSEMBLE who might be passing by.

The detectives finally spot SUNDAY and run towards him, only to watch as he cheerfully escapes in a hot air balloon. The violin finishes playing with a flourish)

GOGOL
Cor.

DE WORMS
Bloody hell.

DR. BULL
I never would have thought a balloon…

MARQUIS
Yes, I'd sooner have expected an elephant than that.

SECRETARY
(angrily) Lost! All is lost!

SYME
Snap out of it! I won't be beaten yet; that blasted thing has to come down somewhere!

(He runs off, looking at the sky. The others follow)

END ACT FOUR, SCENE ONE

Scene Two

(A country road. A tree. Evening. The light of a full moon in a clear sky. The six detectives are sitting, standing, or pacing. All look weary and disheveled. SYME stares at the sky. The SECRETARY sets a lantern on the ground and searches her person for a match)

SECRETARY
(finding none) I'll be hanged. Do any of you have a match?

DE WORMS
What do you suppose we are, a band of bloody dynamiters?

GOGOL
(pulling a match from his pocket and giving it to the SECRETARY) Here you go.

(The SECRETARY accepts the match and lights the lantern. Silence)

DR. BULL
All such rubbish. I can't believe we lost it.

DE WORMS
Why so surprised? I think it's good and bloody
settled that we're the worst bunch of detectives
Scotland Yard could have possibly hoped for.
Naturally we're able to misplace a tremendous
balloon floating through the sky.

GOGOL
If we ever were, y'mean.

DE WORMS
Were?

GOGOL
Detectives. You heard the man; it was him all
along in that black room, handing out his blue
cards and laughing at us; telling us, "You, Boyo,
Go Fight Anarchy!"

SECRETARY
Did you believe all that! Sunday would have said
he was anybody.

GOGOL
Yeah? How'd he know about the dark room?

SECRETARY
Perhaps he knew...because...

MARQUIS
Perhaps he knew about the man in the dark room
because he's already killed him.

(Pause)

DR. BULL
Yet can I confess? I do not find it so hard to think

that Sunday and our lawful superior were in fact one and the same. I would say that I felt exactly the same in the presence of both men—a deep and abiding fear, to be sure, but also a queer sympathy.

SECRETARY
You've gone off your skull.

DR. BULL
I can't explain it, true. And it never stopped me from fighting him like hell! But there were times I looked at Sunday and all I saw was a great mischievous child. A force of Nature; but doesn't nature also play tricks with no seeming rhyme or reason, and do we not always forgive Nature, eventually?

SECRETARY
You do not know Sunday at all. Perhaps it is because you are better than I, and do not know damnation. You did not see Sunday when he was alone, in that musty room he kept as an office. Sitting there, shaking like some monstrous half-formed mass of deep sea lumps and protoplasm, something not quite life but satisfied for that condition. *(Beat)* There was once, I saw him and he seemed to be weeping; his whole body shuddering and I thought: "At least it is something that Sunday can be miserable." And then it broke on me that what I took for sorrow was laughter. That he was laughing at me and all humanity. Do you ask me to forgive him that? It is no small thing to be laughed at by something at once lower and stronger than oneself.

MARQUIS
You exaggerate, madam. He's unsettling, sure,

but Sunday's not quite the circus freak as you make out. The first time I met him it was broad daylight, and he was well-spoken and ordinary. But I'll tell you what is a trifle creepy about him. He's absent-minded. There are times you'll talk to him and his eyes will go blind; he'll forget that you are there, and that is just a bit too awful in a man like Sunday. His is a casual savagery, like that of a cat feeding. Would any of you like to spend ten mortal hours in a room with an absent-minded tiger?

DR. BULL
And what do you think of Sunday, Gogol?

GOGOL
I don't think of Sunday on principle. Any more than I'd stare at the sun at noonday.

DE WORMS
I believe you may all be right. And I also believe you may all be wrong. His is a changing land-scape, Sunday's is. His face is too large, but too loose, and for the sharpness of his features I could never focus on it. In light of everything, I doubt he has a face at all, and so terrible is his power that now I doubt that anybody has a face at all. Is there matter, or just a combination of perspec-tives? What did he say, before he leapt off the balcony? "You cannot arrest me until you know me, and you cannot know me until..." *(Beat)* Small wonder we failed to take him.

SECRETARY
Syme? What's your opinion?

(Pause. SYME continues looking at the sky)

SYME

My opinion…is that we have an awful lot to say about what we know of Sunday, but seem to think nothing of the fact that we don't know each other at all. *(He looks at the others)* All this time we've spent together and all I can think to call each of you is by the names of our respective charades. Sunday is off and we may never know who he was. Who are you?

Pause.

MARQUIS

Ratcliffe. My name is Ratcliffe.

DR. BULL

Harper.

SECRETARY

Payne.

GOGOL

_____. *(insert actor's actual name)*

DE WORMS

Wilks. *(He begins removing his makeup)* And I'll tell you, I don't know why I'm still wearing all of this. I stopped thinking about it. *(To SYME)* And you'd be?

SYME

Me? Gabriel Syme.

DE WORMS

That you are! Very cunning.

SYME

Cunning? How kind of you. But I fear that we find our wits well outmatched by our opponent.

(Beat) You know what I think of Sunday? I think of him as the whole world. When I first saw him, from the street below the balcony, all I saw was the back of him, and from that view I knew instantly; this was the worst human being in the world. The odd thing, though? When I came up to the table, and saw his face, it frightened me not because of its evil, but because, there in the sunlight, he seemed so good. Then he turned again, and he was an animal and I loathed him. But when he turned back again...he was an archangel. This for me has been the mystery of Sunday; the mystery of the whole world—when I see the back, I am sure the noble face is but a mask; when I see the face I know the back is only a jest. Bad is so bad that we cannot but think good an accident; good is so good that we feel certain that evil could be explained. *(Beat)* The secret of the whole world is that we have only known the back of it, the six of us. We see everything from behind and it looks brutal. This isn't a tree, but the back of a tree. The back of the moon, the back of those clouds that Sunday's balloon slipped into. Do you see? Everything, not just us, has been stooping and hiding its face. If we could only get round front...

MARQUIS
You've lost me, Syme.

SYME
That's exactly right. I've lost you, you've lost me, we've lost ourselves and for now we may well be lost to the world. I'll tell you all something else.

DE WORMS
What's that?

SYME
This is no way to fight anarchists.

(Silence. SYME resumes watching the sky. After a moment, a MESSENGER arrives. The detectives all take immediate notice)

MESSENGER
Detectives. I have a message for you.

SECRETARY
From whom?

MESSENGER
I was told you knew his name.

DR. BULL
So he's still alive, then?

MARQUIS
As likely he's dead, just to cheat us. That would be just like one of his larks, if he'd gotten himself killed.

MESSENGER
He wishes you to know that he will be in Saffron Park tomorrow at sunset, and that he requests the honor of your company. If he is in the humor, he says, he may even explain everything.

SECRETARY
May explain everything?

MESSENGER
Those were his words. Good evening, detectives.

MESSENGER exits.

MARQUIS
A trap.

GOGOL
Aye.

DR. BULL
Why don't I feel any fear, then?

SYME
All that is clear to me, is that I don't understand anything, and that this offer of Sunday's fills me with remarkable comfort. I have grown so accustomed to these uncomfortable adventures that the very prospect of a comfortable adventure about knocks me out. *(He yawns)* I think we face that Armageddon that our superior officer warned us of. One shouldn't face that without a proper night's sleep.

(He exits, and the others follow)

END SCENE TWO

Scene Three

(Saffron Park; the same bench where this all began. As before, members of the ENSEMBLE stroll along the sidewalk, talking with each other. SUNDAY is already sitting on the bench, watching this all with amusement. He is eventually left alone onstage.

After a moment, SYME approaches him)

SYME
Sunday. *(Beat)* Good day.

SUNDAY
Good day to you, detective.

SYME
No. No "detective." I stand before you as a poet. A poet of law...but only a poet.

SUNDAY
A pity. You made a fine policeman.

SYME
Said the head anarchist.

SUNDAY
Don't be daft, Syme; if an anarchist's goal is to destroy leadership, how can there ever be a head anarchist? If you'd all have realized that sooner, maybe you could have spared yourselves your ordeal. *(Beat)* I notice the others didn't come with you.

SYME
You notice incorrectly. The others are taking steps to prevent any further escape on your part.

(The other five approach the bench, surrounding SUNDAY on all sides. SUNDAY notes this nonchalantly)

SUNDAY
Shot the horses, did you? Popped the balloons?

MARQUIS
Nothing so drastic. Nonetheless, this time you are caught, villain.

SUNDAY
And what shall you do with me, now that I am caught? Hm? *(Beat)* You should release me, you six, and hunt me again. When will you hounds ever again face such a fox?

GOGOL
Can't speak for the others, guv'nor, but this hound will be content with scraps and bones from here on.

SECRETARY
We ask you again. Who are you?

SUNDAY
Haven't you realized? *(Beat. He speaks in a newly*

serious tone) I am God.

(A long pause. SUNDAY suddenly laughs uproariously)

SUNDAY
Uncanny! Each of you knew immediately that that was a lie and yet! The doubt on your faces! I would pay all the money in all the banks of Britain to see it again! *(Beat)* But I beg your pardon. *(He laughs again)* "I am God!"

DR. BULL
You are not God. Are you the Devil?

SUNDAY
The Devil! Would you have me be the Devil, then? Would that satisfy you?

DR. BULL
Satisfy...would not be the word.

SUNDAY
No. Wouldn't satisfy me, either. What a poor and miserable creature is the Adversary! I far prefer my station to that of Satan.

SYME
And that station would be...

SUNDAY
Sloane Square. And after that, Victoria. Or else Baker Street...

DE WORMS
Enough of your blasted riddles!

SUNDAY
One man's riddle is another man's religion, Mr. Wilks. But your point is taken. *(Beat)* Who am I?

(He draws a blue card from his pocket) Scotland Yard; Anarchist Detail. But there is no Anarchist Detail. There is only me.

MARQUIS
Then who are we?

SUNDAY
You? You are also me. You are false identities and disguises of mine. You are the most convenient of all disguises, because you wear yourselves.

SECRETARY
I won't hear that. I'm my own being, by God, I know who I am and I won't have you accuse me of being something you pull from your wardrobe.

SUNDAY
Is that so…Detective, Secretary, Monday, Payne? Your own being? If you insist.

DR. BULL
I admit I find this disheartening. I had believed I was recruited to fight anarchists.

SUNDAY
And you were! And so you have! Don't you know your own heroic accomplishment? You have dismantled the Supreme Anarchist Council!

DE WORMS
But there wasn't any bloody Supreme Anarchist Council!

SUNDAY
Such the greater accomplishment! You have destroyed something that never existed; not even time can do that. How do you think one goes about fighting anarchists? Hunting them down

and killing them?

GOGOL
That's right. How else do you get the job done,
then? Talking to them? Asking them nicely to stop
being anarchists? Twaddle. You hunt the blighters
down, and you kill them, or else lock them away.
Every last one of them.

SUNDAY
You're as dense as _____ as ever you were as
Gogol, you know that? And I miss your accent. It
provided me a sort of calming amusement. But no
matter. Hunt down and kill every last one, you say.
What do you do with the one that pops up after
you kill the last one? Kill him too, I'd guess. And
the one after him. And the twenty or thirty after
that one. And the hundred beyond those...? *(Beat)*
This is our common mistake; to think that we are
fighting a war against a material enemy, when in
fact our enemy is the anarchy itself, masquerading
as it does in a coat of dynamiters. The idea, you
see! Our enemy is the idea! For how long have we
focused on the hydra's heads without once taking
aim at the heart of the beast?

DE WORMS
And so the destruction of our artificial Council
is...what?

SUNDAY
The rumblings of avalanche. They will whisper
to each other, in the days ahead, that something
terrible has happened. Nobody has heard from
the Supreme Council in weeks, they will say.
There will be a rumor that they have all been
captured and executed. How did you hear this?

How could this happen? Are we compromised, are there detectives among us even now? *(Beat)* And there are not. But let them tear at each other instead of civilization. Let them lose hope in their false god of gunpowder, whose high priests were so easily dispatched!

MARQUIS
You wished to cause a crisis of faith in the anarchists.

SUNDAY
Quite right. Quite right.

(All the detectives save SYME murmur in assent and appreciation)

SYME
A clever plot, to be sure. Commendable. *(Beat)* Forgive me; our current scenery inspires in me a predisposition to argue. I wonder if it was necessary to guide the six of us to stray so close to hell. Since France at least I have been experiencing something of a crisis of faith myself.

SUNDAY
Good. You should feel such things. All who would battle anarchists should understand their terror, their distrust, their isolation. When the anarchist sneers in your face that you have never known agony, you will gaze back, and tell him: "I have known suffering, little man. I have known the oppression of a fly fighting the universe."

SYME
I see. And if you had broken us?

SUNDAY
You were chosen because you would not be. I will admit: There were errors in the early stages. Mistakes made. Your predecessor, Thursday, rather lost his wits toward the end and had to be dispatched. You were not so weak as he. The serious lawmen cannot be broken.

SYME
I am grateful for your trust, sir. But I must question further. We are your serious lawmen, as you say, your most committed lieutenants. Yet rather than use us to our potential, you employed us as mere props in your opera. *(Beat)* And at last I know who you are, Sunday.

SUNDAY
Is that right? Who am I?

SYME
You are an audience. But worse than that; you are that most superior of spectators, that man who sits at the side of chess matches and insists that his years of observation have made him a Grand Master. Our sin, yes, I confess, our sin was to have been action without thought, but yours, sir, is to have been thought without action.

SUNDAY
Without action, Syme? Have these past few days been but theoretical? Or a nightmare, perhaps, from which we will soon awaken, not knowing which of us were mere figments the entire time?

SYME
Look at you. Look at you, Sunday; so taken, so satisfied with your strategy that you are blind to

anything save your own cunning. You aim for the hydra's heart, bravo, jolly good show; while you forget that its heads yet remain! You have us fight from chaos, striking our best blows at your engineered shadows while the threat remains on the field! Incompetence! Sheer and utter incompetence!

SUNDAY
I fail to hear a question in all of this, Syme.

SYME
(furious) My question? My question! My question is this: If your serious lawmen were occupied with watching each other, with unraveling your trickery one thread at a time...who was watching the serious anarchists?

(Pause. For the first time, SUNDAY seems troubled)

SUNDAY
I...

(Everybody except for SYME freezes, momentarily. He speaks to the audience)

SYME
I will remind you, once more: it had been a beautiful day. Clear and cloudless, the sky painted in symphonic shades of blue. (Beat) Remember that.

(The scene resumes. There is suddenly the sound of a horrendous explosion. Then another. And another. The sound of crowds of people wailing in anguish. Members of the ENSEMBLE run by, escaping from the carnage in fear. The detectives are stunned, staring offstage in horror.

GREGORY enters suddenly, running, laughing in

mad triumph. He has his false dynamite in his hand. He does not notice the detectives at the bench)

GREGORY
(yelling offstage) YEEEEESSSSS! Yes, at last! Burn, you great stone souls! Know who at last has pulled you down and made you taste blood! (He turns and sees SUNDAY, and is immediately overcome with an emotion mixing joy and fear) Sunday! Mr. President! Do you see what we have done! (He spots SYME) And you especially, Syme! Do you see? (He starts towards SYME but is restrained by the others. They take his false dynamite from him) Mr. President, I must tell you something, my vows be damned. That man there, the one you anointed Thursday, that man is a detective of Scotland Yard! (He breaks free of the others) Oh yes! But look at how feeble he is, surrounded by our great works! See, Syme! See London burn! See your precious law cowed before our might! See!

(He rushes back to the edge of the stage and raises his arms, watching the chaos offstage. The detectives look at GREGORY and then back to SUNDAY. SUNDAY shows no fear or regret, but all trace of his previously jovial nature has vanished. He is deep in consideration)

SYME
Sir.

SUNDAY
Hm.

SYME
Sir. (Beat) What would you have us do?

SUNDAY
I'm not... *(Beat)* I'm not sure. *(Beat)* I'm not sure how to explain this.

(The detectives look at each other for a moment. They each remove what may be left of their disguises, draw their blue cards and toss all of them at SUNDAY'S feet before rushing off, as one, in the direction of the fire.

SUNDAY is left with GREGORY, who looks at him admiringly.

SUNDAY turns and walks away from the fire)

END OF PLAY

ABOUT THE AUTHOR

Gilbert Keith Chesterton (born May 29, 1874, London, England—died June 14, 1936, Beaconsfield, Buckinghamshire) was an English critic and author of verse, essays, novels, and short stories, known for his exuberant personality and rotund figure.

Interested in literary critisism, social criticism, and theology, Chesterton is best remembered for his literary works, most especially his allegorical **The Man Who Was Thursday** and his **Father Brown** series of detective novels. All in all he wrote over 80 books, several hundred poems, some 200 short stories, 4000 essays, and several plays.

"He is a sane man who can have tragedy in his heart and comedy in his head."

ABOUT THE PLAYWRIGHT

Bilal Dardai is a playwright, essayist, and performance artist who has been based in the Chicago theatrical community since 2000. He is an emeritus ensemble member and artistic director of The Neo-Futurists and a current ensemble member at Lifeline Theatre. He is a regular fixture in Chicago's thriving "live lit" scene, performing essays at The Paper Machete, Write Club, and Salonathon; and he is a contributing scriptwriter to the audio dramas "PleasureTown" and "Unwell." Bilal has been nominated for three Joseph Jefferson Awards and is a past recipient of an Illinois Arts Council Fellowship in Scriptworks.

Sordelet Ink Plays by
Joseph Zettelmaier

It Came From Mars

The Decade Dance

Dr. Seward's Dracula

The Gravedigger
A Frankenstein Play

Campfire

Dead Man's Shoes

The Scullery Maid

All Childish Things

Northern Aggression
(and the creek don't rise)

Ebenezer
A Christmas Play

Stage Fright
A Horror Anthology

For information about production rights, visit:

www.jzettelmaier.com

More Plays From SORDELET INK

A Tale of Two Cities
by Christoper M Walsh
adapted from the novel by Charles Dickens

The Count of Monte Cristo
by Christoper M Walsh
adapted from the novel by Alexandre Dumas

The Moonstone
by Robert Kauzlaric
adapted from the novel by Wilkie Collins

Her Majesty's Will
by Robert Kauzlaric
adapted from the novel by David Blixt

Season on the Line
by Shawn Pfautsch
adapted from Herman Melville's Moby-Dick

Hatfield & McCoy
by Shawn Pfautsch

Once A Ponzi Time
by Joe Foust

Eve of Ides
by David Blixt

Visit www.sordeletink.com for more!